The Melodeon

by Glendon Swarthout

The Melodeon

Glendon Swarthout

Illustrated by Richard Cuffari

Doubleday & Company, Inc., Garden City, New York   1977

Library of Congress Cataloging in Publication Data

Swarthout, Glendon Fred.
The melodeon.

Autobiographical.
1. Swarthout, Glendon Fred—Biography—Youth.
2. Novelists, American—20th century—Biography.
I. Title.
PS3537.W3743Z52   813'.5'2
ISBN: 0-385-06163-3
Library of Congress Catalog Card Number 77-70983

for Ephraim, Sarah,
Will, and Ella . . . may the
music of the melodeon attend
their dreams . . .

melodeon: a small keyboard organ
in which the tones are produced by
drawing air through metal reeds by means
of a bellows operated by pedals.

Webster's New World Dictionary

The Melodeon

ONE

I WRITE THESE LINES IN THE FIFTY-FOURTH YEAR of my life. They begin a tale I might long ago have tried to tell, but an intuition stayed my pen. The time, I sensed, was not yet prime for me. I was neither old enough nor young enough to attempt the story. And so I waited. The years passed. Now, this autumn, as the days wither and the stars recede and another Christmas nears, I am old enough at last to tell it truly, and young enough at last to know what it means.

When I was thirteen years of age I was literally farmed out by my parents. Put on a train in Philadelphia, I was sent west, alone, to live with my mother's father and mother on their farm a few miles south of Howell, in

Michigan. It was not an unusual exile then. Those were
the 1930s, the decade of an unexampled American de-
pression, and thousands of parents, unable to support
their children, begged foster-homes for them with more
prosperous relatives. My father had lost his job, for
months had walked the streets in vain seeking another,
and his relief payments of ten dollars a week did not
suffice to pay rent and raise a growing youngster. Or-
phaned by economics, I had to go. I was fortunate to
have a farm to go to, for farmers, everyone said, were
luckier than most. No matter how hard the times, they always had enough to eat.

I went to live with Will and Ella Chubb, my mater-
nal grandparents. Their farm was half a section home-
steaded and cleared by Will's grandfather, a man named
Major who came west in a covered wagon from York
State in 1836, before Michigan became a state. The land
had been kind to Major Chubb, and his son Ephraim, and
Ephraim's son Will, good farmers as their Yorkshire fore-
bears had been before them. There were twenty-acre
fields now, and fox-squirrel woods and green pastures for
the sheep and a huckleberry marsh and a lake, deep and
blue and troubled with pickerel. There was a barn, with
haymow above and sheepshed and horse stalls and
cowshed underneath, to which was attached a chickenhouse. A large granary stored the harvests and a treasury
of machinery—thresher, tractor, corn binder, wheat
binder, disc harrow, oat drill, hay drag, hayrake, tedder,
mowing machine, plows, ensilage cutter, cornhusker,
stoneboat, reaper, cultivator, flat drag, spring-tooth drag,
and several wagons. The house itself was white frame,

with acetylene lights, a bathroom, a screened porch, a parlor with a pump-organ, and a feather-tick bed in my very own room upstairs. If one had to be, I soon decided, this was a neat place to be an orphan.

I did my best to deserve it. I wore overalls. I walked three miles to and three from the one-room schoolhouse next to the church at Chubb's Corners, where another boy and I constituted the seventh grade. After school I helped Will, my grandfather. I learned to hitch and unhitch the team, to fork shocks into the ensilage cutter at silo-filling time, to pick Sheepsnose and Baldwin apples in the orchard and assist at the cider-press. I tried milking, but simply couldn't get the grip of it. The fact was, I was thirteen, all arms and legs and thumbs, and a city boy, and much less a menace to others and udders when I did domestic chores for Ella, my grandmother.

I dried the dishes.

I split kindling and fetched wood for the Majestic cookstove in the kitchen.

I separated. In the woodshed, behind the kitchen, stood a cylinder of steel with two spouts and a wooden handle. You poured pails of milk fresh from the faucet into the open top, placed a milk can under one spout and a cream bucket under the other, bent your back, braced your shoes, laid both hands on the handle, and began to crank. You cranked your arms almost out of the sockets. I had no idea what went on inside the separator, but considerable did, for a growl commenced to emanate from the rig which, as you revolved the handle faster and faster, increased in pitch and volume to a howl, then to a scream. It was a fatiguing yet exciting operation. Milk streamed from one spout, cream from the other, and sound assailed the ears, a deafening, melodramatic music appropriate to any number of swashbuckle scenes.

You could crank and crank and close your eyes and be at sea in a typhoon, masts toppling as you fought the wheel to keep your schooner's bow into the wind.

You could be a fearless cowboy galloping to the rescue of the heroine, spurred by her shriek as she clung to the edge of a cliff.

My favorite fantasy, though, while cranking and puffing and separating, was that I was spinning the prop of my silver monoplane, "The Spirit of St. Louis," taking off from Long Island, then clutching the controls as the engine droned us over the dark Atlantic until we landed, the eyes of the world upon us, at Le Bourget.

And always, always, there were eggs. Ella kept two hundred chickens. "Good layers," she called them—a characteristically rural understatement. Those Leghorns of hers were cornucopias, mother-lodes, veritable volcanoes of eggs. Evidently they never left the nest long enough to cackle, scratch, or cluck, for I gathered, washed, and crated hen fruit till I couldn't face it boiled, fried, or scrambled on my breakfast plate. By a neighbor Ella sent two crates to a grocer in Howell each week. They brought eight to twelve cents a dozen, and her egg money she divided evenly—half for staples she needed and a half to be hoarded for an automobile.

It was a source of shame and bitterness to her that the Chubbs were the only family thereabouts without one. The Cadwells, down the road, trucked her crates to town in a Model A, the Stackables had a Nash, even Joe and Abby Henshaw strutted a Model T. Odd by end,

while drying dishes, I learned that three years previously, when she had her husband almost at the point of investing in a car, a smooth-talking salesman had persuaded him instead to trade in his old tractor for an expensive new Rumely OilPull. That was the beginning of payments and the end of the automobile. Will was pitifully "soft on machinery," she confided, excluding cars, which in his opinion were only fuss-budget horseless carriages. This tragic flaw in him had kept them machinery-poor throughout their married life, and though she had put her foot down about indoor plumbing, a bathroom with tub and facilities, they still made do with an acetylene lighting system, the only one in a neighborhood elegant with electricity.

And so she saved half her egg money for a Studebaker. When I asked what was wrong with a Ford, she said nothing, but an advertised feature of the Studebaker was "Free Wheeling." She believed the latter implied that you could get up speed, turn off the ignition, and coast for miles, thereby using little or no gasoline. The thrift of it appealed to her. But when I argued that you could buy a heck of a lot of gas for the difference in price between a Ford and a Studie, Ella pursed her lips and dismissed the matter. She would not admit to inconsistency. She was a woman.

That was my problem. She was not supposed to be. She was supposed to be a grandmother. I didn't know Will and Ella well when I arrived at the farm, for I had visited them only twice as a child. It took me till Christmas to comprehend that they were human beings, and to love them deeply as such. "Grandparents," meanwhile, was an easier category to handle. A boy could crank humanity through his consciousness and easily separate "grandparents" from "people." Grandparents were old. They were a little unreal, like actors in a play. They might have been young once, have loved and hated and grieved, been weak and stubborn and inconsistent, might have known fear and passion, rage and wonder, might have sung to churning and kissed their own raw earth in ecstasy, but this foolishness they had long ago forgotten.

Yes, I was convinced until Christmas that grandparents were gray and kind and frail and full of legend and soon to die, and that was all.

TWO

IT WAS AN EVENTFUL AUTUMN. THE CHURCH AT Chubb's Corners burned down in October. Electricity had just been installed, and faulty wiring was probably responsible. But the men of the congregation, farmers every one, set to work on Sundays and in rainy weather and by the first of December, in time to beat the snow, a new church was built. Money for materials was hard to come by—Ella, I think, gave at least an arm and a leg of a Studebaker—and while the frame structure was unpainted on the outside and unfinished on the in, and lacked lighting, it had a pulpit and a wood stove for heat and benches for pews. The Lord, the Reverend Ledwidge assured his small flock at the first service, would be pleased.

The second event was Will's coming in from the barn Thanksgiving eve and informing us that one of his old ewes was pregnant. "Don't believe me," he added. "I don't believe it myself. But she is. Four months along, I calculate."

"What's so impossible?" I inquired.

"Sheep," he said, "never lamb in the winter. I know. I've kept sheep for forty years. Lambs are dropped in April, May, or June."

"If I was a ewe," said I with urban impudence, "I'd drop a lamb any old time I wanted to."

He looked at me and tugged an end of his mustache. Will had a luxuriant brush which drooped at each corner of his mouth. He called it his "tea-strainer," because when he drank green tea from a saucer he could strain the leaves through it, so that the appurtenance was useful as well as distinguished. "No," said he, "if you were a ewe you'd get around to lovering when you and the ram were ready. Would you like me to explain?"

My grandmother hopped over that indelicate puddle quickly. "Maybe we'll have a lamb born for Christmas— wouldn't that be nice?" she said, putting the morning oatmeal on the stove so as not to waste the overnight heat. "Now that I think of it, Will, I've seen pictures on calendars, of the Christ child in the manger, with Mary and Joseph, and there's usually a lamb nearby, and that was Christmas. So lambs must have been born in the winter back then."

"Those pictures were painted by painters," stated her husband.

"Well?" she challenged.

"Painters," he said with finality, "do not keep sheep."

The third event was something which didn't happen. It didn't snow. The days were gray, November turned cold, skim ice appeared upon the lake, and Will put a barrel of cider in the back yard, but there was no snow. The neighbors mentioned it at every meeting and over the party line on the telephone. The winter wheat would suffer.

But it was winter now, unmistakably, and Christmas neared. I pined. A time or two, walking home from school, I shed a tear. I wrote my father and mother every other day rather than every week.

The barrel of cider froze over. Will chunked out the ice and let it refreeze, chunked out the ice and let it refreeze, again and again. When there were but a few inches of clear liquid at the bottom, he clasped the barrel fondly to his chest and carried it into the basement.

He studied the old ewe from every angle, he felt her woolly sides, he shook a skeptical head, but she was irrefutably pregnant.

Then, the day before the day before Christmas, it snowed, a light frosting on a cake, and stopped.

When we woke the next morning, however, our world whirled with snow. A real blinger of a blizzard came down upon us out of Canada. I gathered the eggs in the afternoon, but the day was so dark and the flakes so thick that, stumbling knee-deep in snow already, I located the house only by its lights. I wore a corduroy flap-cap, with the flaps down over my ears, yet the wind almost tore it from my head. Will declared he had never seen such a storm.

At supper, Ella said her customary grace. "Dear Lord, bless this food to our use and us to Thy service," she murmured, then added a postscript: "And let the storm pass so that we may worship Thee tomorrow. Amen." The next day, Christmas, fell on Sunday that year, and my grandmother never missed church. For dessert that evening she had made a three-layered shortcake filled and topped with black raspberries she had picked from her patch in August and canned. The Lord may have blessed the food to our use, but I am sure He envied us that black raspberry shortcake.

Will went to the barn again after supper to see to his expectant ewe. Usually I dried the dishes and Ella washed, but tonight I volunteered to do them all while she prepared a hen for tomorrow's dinner, scalding the bird and plucking and drawing it, then setting it to cool overnight in the woodshed. In the morning she would pinfeather, stuff, and truss it, and roast it while we were at church. I had mixed emotions about a chicken for Christmas dinner. Turkey was traditional, though I knew she could not afford one. On the other hand it would be gratifying, during dinner, to reflect that there was one less good layer on the assembly line.

"As long as I live," said my grandmother out of a clear blue sky, "I'll never understand your grandfather."

I accepted that. If you had been married to a man for forty-six years and still didn't understand him, you probably never would.

"I told you," she went on, "he's soft on machinery."

"Yes." I paid her only partial attention. To do the dishes by yourself was a chore and a half. Using the pump beside the sink, I had filled a dishpan and teakettle and put them on the stove, and both were boiling now.

"He can't even bring himself to kill a hen."

"He can't?"

"I have to do it myself, always have. And he's certainly soft on the neighbors."

"How come?" I lugged the dishpan to the sink and set to work, dispirited by a tower of baking pans in addition to the dishes.

"Why, everyone around here owes him for the summer threshing—and last summer's, too," she said. "That's how he justified buying a new tractor. 'I'll do the threshing for the whole township,' he told me, 'so much a bushel, and that way we'll pay off the tractor and you can have a car to boot.' And I let him. And what happened? They didn't pay a penny last summer and they haven't this and they don't intend to."

She plucked fiercely. I clattered loudly.

"Why not?" I asked.

"Because wheat's down to twenty-eight cents a bushel, so they're all storing it in hopes of a better price. If he'd only ask them to pay something, even a little, I know they could, most of them. But he won't. 'Times are hard,' he'll say, 'and they're my friends. Ella, I can't do it.' That's what I mean—soft."

"Oh," I said.

"But he can be as stubborn as a mule, too. When that ewe drops her lamb, you watch. He'll insist it isn't a lamb at all, because it's the wrong time of year." She put heart, gizzard, and liver away in a bowl for eventual gravy. "I'll give you another example. Did you know that when he was six years old he could play the organ beautifully?"

"He could?"

"But when he heard his father was dead he stopped and never played another note?"

That stopped me. "He didn't? Why not?"

"Stubborn," she replied. "His mother begged him, she told me so, but he never would. That's what I mean— hard and soft at the same time. I'll never understand him if I live to be a hundred."

I rinsed from the teakettle and stood there thinking and drying. Some of the family history I knew, my mother had told me. Ephraim Chubb went away to the war with the 10th Michigan Cavalry from this very farm in 1863. His young wife, my great-grandmother Sarah, received a letter in 1864 saying that he was missing in action. Sarah waited, as did her small son Willy, who had never seen his father. Five years later, in 1869, she got a second letter from the War Department. Ephraim's remains had been plowed up near Strawberry Plains, Tennessee. He had been killed on a raid, and interred hastily by his comrades. He was shipped home to Sarah, who buried him in the Putnam Township ground near the church at Chubb's Corners.

"Maybe that's why he never played it again," I speculated. "I mean, after he found out his father was dead instead of missing. Maybe his heart was broken."

"Fiddlesticks," she said. It was her only expletive.

In a few minutes we heard Will enter the woodshed and stomp the snow from his boots. I finished the dishes, Ella the hen, he came into the kitchen and warmed himself at the stove and said he'd never seen such a storm and the ewe was due in the next hour or two, then Ella said we had just time to have the tree before the phone rang. That was to be my Christmas present from my parents—a telephone call. We had planned it in our letters. They had given up their telephone, but would go to a friend's house and call me at precisely eight o'clock, and we could talk precisely three minutes. So the three of us went into the living room.

The tree was a tall one—Will and I had cut it ourselves, in the huckleberry marsh—and while it lacked the number of ornaments I was accustomed to at home, Ella and I had strung about a mile of popcorn. And when she lit the tiny candles, the tree was lovely. There were only two presents, both for me. My grandfather's was a walnut-handled pocketknife, my grandmother's a scarf she had knitted, long enough to wind round and round.

"Gee, thanks a lot," I said. "They're really swell. I don't have anything for you, though. I don't know how to make anything and I didn't have any money."

"Why, you're our gift, James," said Ella, and kissed me on the cheek.

Will put a hand on my shoulder. "We haven't had a pup around here for a dog's age."

We wished each other Merry Christmas, then pinched the candles out and returned to the kitchen, for it was nearly eight o'clock.

They sat at the table and I stood by the wall phone. Our ring was three long and one short, and after five minutes I decided some of the garrulous wives in the neighborhood must be on the line, so I lifted the receiver and listened in. Universal sin absolves individuals, and since everyone did it in those days, listening in on a party line was not considered sinful. But the line hummed and I hung up the receiver.

Wood hissed in the stove. Over the table the clock

ticked. We tried not to look at it. Wind boxed the house. Under us, the joists creaked with cold. For once, we three were lonely.

"Just imagine," said Ella, crocheting a potholder and making conversation. "A body speaking to someone in Michigan all the way from Philadelphia. Whatever will they think of next?"

"A night like this, maybe the lines are down," Will suggested.

His wife frowned at him.

"Now when they call," he said to me, making amends, "don't fritter your time away having us talk to them. We can write. It's your present and you use every blamed second of it."

"Thank you," I said. My palms were damp. I was developing a lump in my throat.

When the phone finally did ring, and we held our breath counting three long and one short, I seized the receiver and could scarcely say hello. The lump in my throat was as big as an egg with a double yolk. Then the sound of my mother's voice broke the egg and me with it. She warned me at the outset that she was watching the clock and three minutes was all they could manage, and that rendered me even more inarticulate. To this day I cannot recall what we said, but I can guess. I determined that she and my father were well. She ascertained from me that I was well and so were Will and Ella. The weather in Philadelphia was clear. We were having a blizzard. My father, to whom I next talked, had not yet found a job. One of Will's sheep was about to have a lamb. I had a dandy new jackknife and scarf. These revelations were followed by a long and excruciating pause, after which we were wishing each other a Merry Christmas and they were saying goodbye and I heard a click and hung the receiver on the hook and couldn't turn around because my eyes were swimming.

"I have an idea," said my grandmother briskly and immediately. "Why don't we go into the parlor and I'll play the melodeon and we'll sing a carol or two?"

I swallowed hard, still facing the phone. "I didn't know you could play."

"I can't very well any more," she confessed. "I make so many mistakes—my fingers, the arthritis you know. That's why I never do. But I used to. Sarah taught me, Will's mother." She put down her crocheting. "Anyway, I'm game if you are."

She nodded at her husband and I tagged after them through the living room, where they opened the sliding doors, and on into the parlor. Will turned up the gas, struck a match, and we had light. I looked at the melodeon as though for the first time.

I wish to describe it in detail. The organ was thirty-three inches high, forty inches wide, and twenty-one inches deep. The wood was cherry. It had a hinged top which folded up and back and became a music rack, revealing a five-octave keyboard and above it, in gilt lettering on the fall-board, the name of the manufacturer: "Mason & Hamlin." Inside the hinged top was stamped the number of the instrument: "10905." At the base were two ten-inch-wide pedals which were pumped alternately to fill the bellows, and they were covered with needlepoint in a floral design. The covering was faded and frayed with use. At the left of the pedals a small wooden treadle protruded. It was called a "swell," or a "loud and soft damper." To raise and lower volume, one depressed it with the left foot while double-pedaling with the right. There was also a bench, covered with the same design in needlepoint, but made of a different wood. It was a handsome instrument, the rich finish unmarred and perfectly preserved. Ella provided me later with another piece of information. The needlepoint coverings for both pedals and bench had been done by Sarah, my great-grandmother, in 1911, the year of her death, and by coincidence the very year Mason & Hamlin discontinued the manufacture of melodeons.

Ella folded back the top, sat down, began to pump, and played several carols, singing along with Will and me. We sang "Silent Night, Holy Night," "We Three Kings of Orient Are," and started "It Came Upon the Midnight Clear." My grandmother hit a few black keys when she should have white, and when I glanced at her fingers on the keyboard, again as though for the first time, I saw that they were gnarled by arthritis, and I understood why she played but seldom. She pumped with vigor, though. We sang with zeal. We ignored the occasional dissonance. The tones of the melodeon were true as ever, and faintly elegiac. The union of their two old voices with my soprano, which would not change to tenor for another year, was not unharmonious. But something gave me gooseflesh. Other presences seemed to join us in the parlor on that Christmas Eve. Other voices, quavery and distant, seemed to swell our choir. It had never occurred to me that ghosts could sing.

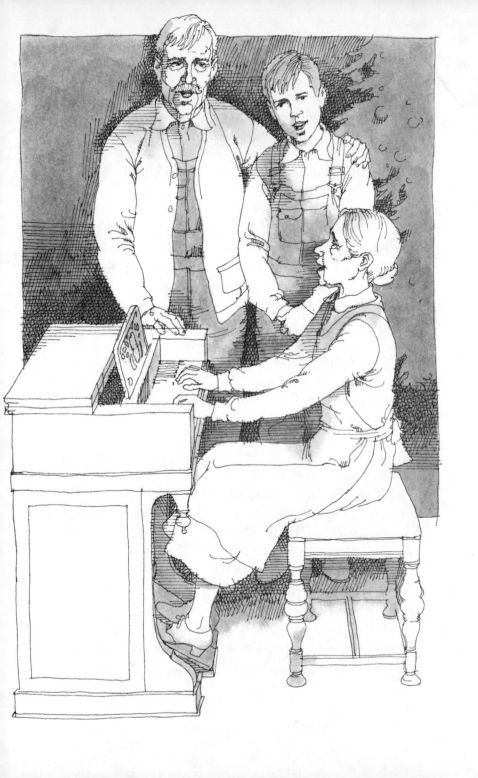

I have said that we started "It Came Upon the Midnight Clear." Suddenly my grandmother stopped.

"Oh, Will!" she whispered.

We waited, mouths open.

"Will!" she said. "I've just had the most wonderful notion!"

We waited, mouths open.

"The melodeon—let's give it to the church for Christmas!"

We closed our mouths. She rose from the bench. Behind the lenses of her spectacles her eyes were wide. Her words spilled. "They haven't even a piano—it would help the singing so much. I never play it—and you won't. Why don't we give it to the church?"

Will tugged his mustache. "No harm in it, I expect."

"Tomorrow's Sunday and Christmas both—we'll surprise them—when they come in, there it will be!"

"Tomorrow?"

"What better time, Chrismas morning?"

He shook his head. "Ella, you forget. This blizzard. I couldn't haul it there tonight."

"Can't you take the team? With a wagon?"

He smiled as though at a child. "There'll be drifts three feet deep in another hour. No team could—"

"If you wanted to, you could," she accused.

He sobered. "I want to," he said, "but I just plumb can't. Not in a month of Sundays could—"

"Fiddlesticks!"

"Girl," he said, "I hate to disappoint you, but there won't even be a service tomorrow. I didn't want to tell you. The roads will be drifted full."

She turned away from us. She lowered the hinged top of the melodeon over the keyboard. "If only we had an automobile," she muttered.

That angered him. "No damned automobile would get there either! Not even a damned Studebaker!"

"How would you know, Will Chubb?" she demanded. "You've never owned one!"

I held my tongue. I was embarrassed and incredulous. In my four months on the farm I had never heard them say a cross word to each other. Old men were not supposed to call old ladies "girl." Even more shocking, grandparents were not supposed to quarrel, ever, and especially on Christmas Eve.

Will glared at his wife's intractable back, then glared at me, then nodded at the doors. I accompanied him through the house into the kitchen.

"I'm going to the barn," he said gruffly. "Have you ever seen anything born?"

"No. No, I haven't."

"Do you want to?"

"Gee, I don't know."

"Make up your mind. I don't know what in Hades that old ewe will have—fish or fowl or a two-headed Hottentot from Timbuctoo—but she can't have a lamb. Not this time of year, she can't. Well?"

"I guess so," I said. "O.K.," I said.

"Then get a move on."

I took my new scarf and we stepped into the woodshed and pulled on our galoshes and stuffed pant legs inside and buckled them up and put on heavy jackets and dropped the flaps of our caps. We lit two kerosene lan-

terns and got them burning clean and each of us carried
one. He lifted his, illumined our faces, and scowled.

"Females," he said.

Since I did not know whether he referred to wives or
ewes, and had in any case little experience with either, I
let my silence concur.

We went out into the storm.

THREE

I HAD NEVER BEEN OUT IN SUCH A NIGHT. I WOUND my scarf round and round my head, binding my face to the eyes, but even then a net of wind-thrown snow tangled my eyelashes. The storm was like a scythe, swinging its cutting edge down out of Canada into Michigan and slashing the forehead, its point stabbing the lining of the lungs. Without the scarf over my nose I doubted if I could draw breath. Without his lantern to guide on, I could never have followed my grandfather to the barn.

We slid the door open wide enough to pass through, entered, stomped snow from our galoshes and slapped it off each other's jackets with our mittens. We were on the barn floor, the haymows rising on either side of us. Walking to the far end, we went halfway down a flight of steps and sat down to overlook the sheepshed. Below and around us a hundred sheep, wearing heavy winter gray, lounged about on yellow straw and considered us as calmly as we considered them.

"Which one?" I asked, unwinding my scarf.

"There." Will pointed at a ewe who lay near the foot of the steps. As I stared at her she stood up, then lay down again. She was restless.

"How'll we know when she's going to have it?"

"We'll know."

"Well, what do we do now?"

"Meditate."

We raised the ear-flaps of our caps. It was warmer inside the sheepshed than out, but our breathing still made little fogs before our faces. I peered until I found the horns of Calvin, the ram. They had a beautiful curl, and he knew it. He was a registered Rambouillet, and had a long, complicated name on his papers, but for short Will called him Calvin in honor of Mr. Coolidge. Neither the ram nor the former President spoke very often, he explained, but when they did, they were worth heeding.

"I wonder what sheep think about," I said.

"Females," was the answer.

"Females?"

"Yes. The contrariness of the critters. Isn't it just like a female to drop a lamb in the middle of a winter night when a man might better be in bed? And isn't it just like a female to expect a man to haul a pump-organ three miles through a snowstorm? I don't understand 'em, you don't understand 'em, and neither does Calvin. Why can't they have their blasted lambs and notions in the spring-time? Why do they keep us men forever out of kilter?"

These were rhetorical questions. After a time he said, "Any damned automobubble ever invented would foun-der in those drifts."

I held my face and hands.

A bit later he said, "I intended to buy one in Twenty-eight, but traded for the OilPull instead. Then I intended to buy one in Twenty-nine, with the threshing money, and you know what happened in Twenty-nine."

The old ewe stood up, then lay down again.

In a while Will said, "She hasn't played that thing in three years. That organ."

I concentrated on Calvin. He was chewing some-thing and being very nonchalant about the drama which was presently to unfold, a theatrical for which he bore in large part the responsibility of authorship.

"You can't get blood out of a turnip," my grandfather said, again to himself. "You can't ask friends and neigh-bors for money when they don't have it. These are sad times. They're fine people. They'll pay when they can."

I felt obliged to change the course of his soliloquy. "I'm sorry you had an argument," I said. "It was my fault, I guess. If I hadn't been here, she wouldn't have played the melodeon, and if she hadn't played, she might not have got the idea."

"Oh, we spat," he said.

"You do?"

"Don't your ma and pa go at it now and again?"

"Well, sure, but they're younger. I didn't think—"

"Old folks fight? Well, they do, sonny. Scratch and

bite as much as ever, and love as much as ever. You have to take the vinegar with the honey. That's marriage for you."

"Oh."

The old ewe stood up and lay down again. She was making me restless. "Guess I'll go give the team some extra hay," I said. "It's Christmas Eve."

"Why not? They didn't have black raspberry short-cake for supper tonight."

Another reason why I wanted to make myself scarce was that, as the delivery drew nigh, I grew less and less inclined to witness it. I hadn't a glimmering what to expect, but whatever might happen, I was convinced I was too young and pure as yet to be exposed to the barn-based facts of life. I might have bad dreams. I might never again be able to look a ewe in the face.

Taking a lantern, I went upstairs and used it to light a look at Tom and Dolly in their stalls below. Both were standing, sound asleep, and presumably cold and hungry. I pitched three forkfuls of hay from the mow down the chute for each of them, which woke them up, and I could hear them crunching and munching gratefully. They were amiable, hard-working horses, and I liked them collectively, as a team, although Tom had too prominent a backbone. I had ridden him once, and bouncing up and down on his spinal column had nearly divided my allegiance.

I wished them both a Merry Christmas and descended again into the sheepshed. "My gosh," I said, "hasn't she had it yet?"

"She will when she's a mind to," said my grandfather.

"Well, I wish she'd shake a leg."

I took my post on the stairsteps again. The old ewe stood up and lay down. I had to think about something else, so I asked Will where the melodeon had come from. Instead of a simple answer, I got another helping of family history, and this time a chapter my mother had not told me, perhaps because she had never heard it herself.

One day in April, in the year 1863, my great-grand-mother Sarah was standing at her kitchen window watching her husband, Ephraim, plowing in a nearby field. Suddenly he stopped, dropped the reins, left the team, and walked toward the house. He had never done that before —once he started a furrow he finished it—and although she was a very young wife, married only two years, Sarah knew in her soul what her husband would say when he reached the house. But she didn't cry or faint or anything, she merely held on hard to a pot in which she was soaking beans. Sarah Chubb waited. Ephraim Chubb walked. He entered the kitchen. They were forming a cavalry regiment around Howell, he said without preliminary, and if she were willing, he wanted to enlist. It would tear him in two to leave her, he said, but he wouldn't be gone long, the Johnnies would soon be whipped, he would get her a hired man to work the place, and if she could manage the separation, he could manage the war. It had been on his conscience, he told her. It had afflicted his dreams. He loved her, but he loved the Union, too, and he revered Mr. Lincoln. He was young and able-bodied and he believed it his duty to get in a lick for his country while he could.

"What did she say?" I asked.

"She said yes. Of course he ought to go. A man

should do what he believed in. It was what she didn't say that cost her."

"What was that?"

"That she was carrying me."

"You?"

"She was two months along with me. If she'd told him that, he'd never have left her. But she didn't tell, and let him go, and that must have cost her plenty. She was a brave woman."

Outside, the storm prowled the walls of the barn. It cried like an animal seeking shelter.

"But what about the melodeon?" I asked.

"Oh. Yes," he said. "Well, he joined up in the cavalry. A week later they brought that organ down from the store in Howell in a wagon. He'd bought it on his way to the war. It was his thank-you to her for letting him go. Not knowing about me, I expect he thought it would keep her company. Sarah could play the piano, so she picked up the organ in no time. Then years later, when she was living with us, she taught Ella how."

"And you how," I added.

"Yes. I wanted to play for him when he came home."

"But he never did. I know that part of it." I kept prying, like the wind beyond the barn walls. "How come, after you found out he was dead, you never played it again?"

He looked at me with such intensity that I wished I hadn't asked. "Because my pa would never hear me," he said. "Nor would he ever see me, nor I him. Reason enough?"

"Sure," I said, turning away from his look. I had not

realized that loss could be so long-lived. I had not known that tears, like flowers pressed between the pages of a book, could be indefinitely preserved. I tried to imagine how I would feel if I had never seen my father, and couldn't, and did not want to. Boys were not supposed to be morbid. Grandparents were not supposed to grieve.

So I turned away, and concentrated on the dilatory ewe, and did not want to do that either. For she continued to stand up and lie down, stand up and lie down, and suddenly she let out a bleat, not of anticipation but of distress. I almost jumped out of my skin.

"Holy Toledo!" I was on my feet. "What's the matter with her now?"

"She's due."

I grabbed my lantern. "Guess I'll just go and check the chickens."

"Afraid they'll lay snowballs tomorrow?"

"Just call me 'Chicken Inspector'!" was my retort. I walked across the sheepshed and into the chickenhouse next door. It was quite a sight to see two hundred hens and several roosters perched on poles, dead to the world. Facing me row upon row, they resembled a somnolent, even an impolite audience, and it seemed appropriate to shake them up with a few remarks. I put down the lantern and struck an elocutionary pose.

"Ahem," I began. "Ladies and gentlemen, it gives me great pleasure to address you tonight. But since the hour is late, and it's colder than a welldigger's clavicle, I will be brief. You have a reputation as 'good layers,' a reputation you labor daily to uphold. Well, I have a word to the wise." I drew a deep breath.

"Lay off!" I roared.

Not an eye opened, not a feather turned.

"Slow down, take it easy," I advised. "Rome wasn't built in a day. A Studebaker isn't bought in a week. Cut your output. Enjoy life a little. Look around. Appreciate nature. Make friends. Whistle a tune. And let's show a little talent. Try to be artists, not machines. See if you can knock out some hard-boiled product, and some soft-boiled. Take a crack at some Easter eggs, nicely decorated. Because I warn you." I gave them a voice of doom. "It doesn't make a doggone bit of difference whether you wear yourselves out or not. No matter how hard you strain, someday for your reward my grandmother will take you to the chopping block and powww!"

I paused for effect, but I might as well have addressed the United States Congress for all the effect I achieved. Nary a rooster squawked in horror, nary a hen went pale at the prospect. These were really dumb chickens.

"That concludes my remarks, ladies and gents," I said. "I wish you a Merry Christmas and I now depart." I bowed low, took up the lantern, and departed.

But even before I reached the sheepshed I heard the old ewe over the storm. There was no mistaking the piteous sound she made. She was in serious trouble.

FOUR

WILL KNELT BESIDE HER IN THE STRAW. SHE WAS lying on her side with her hind legs stretched out and bawling her head off. Every animal in the flock, even Calvin, was standing now, concerned.

"What's wrong?" I asked.

"I don't know. Something. She's trying, but she can't. Something amiss."

He had taken off his cap. Now he laid hands on her sides, pressing, examining.

"Maybe there's a leg tucked up. That happens. Or maybe it's a breech."

"What's that?"

"Lamb the wrong way to. The hind end first. Should

be head first." My grandfather sat back on his haunches. "I can't tell. I wish I could."

He bit on a knuckle. I had never seen him so upset. Cold as it was, there were beads of sweat on his forehead. Finally he removed his jacket and rolled up his right shirt-sleeve and the underwear beneath it to the elbow.

"What're you going to do?"

"Reach into her."

I went weak. "Oh jeepers no," I blurted.

"Have to. Or we'll lose her and the lamb both."

"Oh my gosh," I said. "But what can you do?"

"If it's a leg, untuck it. If it's a breech, turn the lamb on its axis. I've done it before. Sometimes it works, sometimes not."

I gritted my teeth. "Any way I can help?"

"Yes. Comfort her."

"Comfort her?"

"Sit down and take her head in your lap. She's in bad pain."

"O.K.," I said. "If I have to," I said.

I had never wanted to do anything less. I was sorry for her, but I didn't know what she might do in her suffering, bite me or kick me or what. Cautiously I sat down on the straw close to the ewe and put an arm around her neck and pulled her head into my lap.

"Now old girl," my grandfather said. He came to his knees between her hind legs. "Now let's see."

I had a last look around. The scene in the shed did make me think of a picture on a calendar—the halos of the lanterns, the beaten gold of the straw, the figures of the flock standing, silent, an old man kneeling by one of the animals as though in prayer. But then I thought of the predicament we were in, the three of us, and it was too much for me. I squinched my eyes shut. Suddenly the ewe bawled louder than ever, and reared her head, and to hold her I had to throw both arms around her neck and hug her against my face.

"Please, old girl, hold still," I begged, my nose full of the waxen smell of her fleece. "There, there, old girl, we can do it. There."

An hour passed, or a minute, and then, just as suddenly she relaxed, and I was sure she must be dead.

"There, by Jehu," I heard my grandfather say.

I could not open my eyes. "What happened?" I choked.

"She had a lamb, that's what."

"Is it all right?"

"Fine and dandy."

I peeked. He was cutting the cord with a loop of binder twine and swabbing red off something small with a fistful of straw. I squinched shut again.

"A Christmas lamb," Will said. "I will be damned."

"I'll be damned," I echoed.

"You can let go of her now," he said. "She wants her kidlet."

I released her head and stood up and opened my eyes. Will laid the lamb, which was all bunched up, on the straw by its mother, and she stretched her neck and commenced at once to lick it. I took one look and sort of wobbled to the stairs and sat down bump and with a forearm wiped the sweat from my own forehead. I was limp as a dishrag. It wasn't that I was innocent or ignorant. I had a general grasp of the theory of birth, but I had been vague, and glad to be, about the nuts and bolts. Now I knew how a lamb was born, and therefore how Ephraim, Sarah, Will, Ella, my father, my mother, and I were born —yes, even I. We had come into the world in agony and struggle and bright blood, and something else, something akin to exaltation. For when I looked at my grandfather he was rolling down his sleeve and grinning ear to ear at me. I stood up and grinned back at him and felt enormously mature and alive. If the two of us had smoked cigars, and anyone had handed them out, we would have smoked like stoves.

Crack!

Without warning, Will smote a palm with a fist. "The OilPull!"

I stood there.

He cracked his palm again. "The OilPull!"

It was clear as mud to me.

He yanked on his jacket, clapped on his cap, faced me with eyes blazing, and said, "James, my boy, do you think we could get it started?"

"The tractor? Why?"

"To haul the organ!"

"Where?"

"To the church!"

"Oh," I said. "Oh!" I said. "Why not?"

"Because it's never been run in the winter. Because I've never seen or heard of one run in the winter, that's why. But if we could start it, boy—drifts be damned! We could haul anything in Christendom anywhere!"

"Sure we can!" I cried, catching his excitement like a fever. "We can do anything!"

"Hold your horses," he cautioned. "A lamb's not a

tractor. Even if we did, it's three long miles and a fearful night. Think we're up to it?"

"Sure we are," I asserted.

"I'm no spring chicken any more."

"I'll help you."

"That's a mighty valuable piece of wood, that organ."

"We'll be careful."

"It tells in the manual how to start it in cold weather —I've read how. But reading's a damn sight different from doing."

"We'll learn as we go along."

"And then there's Ella. It's got to be a surprise or it isn't worth a pinch of dried owl dung."

"We won't tell her."

"But she's a light sleeper. And you can hear that Oil-Pull from here to Dee-troit."

I had no way around that.

"It's not like falling off a log," he warned me. He was having a lot of second thoughts. "We'd better sit a spell and meditate."

We sat down on the steps again. I chewed on a stem of straw. Will tugged the ends of his mustache. Taking up the immemorial tasks of motherhood, the old ewe continued to lick her lamb. And now that the show was over, the flock lay down again and drowsed into ovine oblivion. Calvin, however, stayed awake with us, savoring his cud and pondering, I imagined, the obligations of paternity. I knew what was expected of me. Along with Will, it was my duty to assay the project and decide if it was feasible or in fact nuttier than a fruitcake. The question was, could an old man and his thirteen-year-old grandson start a tractor on a below-zero Christmas Eve, and if so, could they then, unbeknownst to wife and grandmother, transport by means of said tractor a melodeon three miles through a blizzard to a church in time for Sunday morning service?

"She may not play it, but she loves that pumper," Will reflected aloud. "It'll cost her to give it away."

This question involved another: how old was old? I knew Will had the sand, but did he have the stamina? He must be in his late sixties at least, I reckoned, and men that age had at least one foot in the grave, and more likely a leg. What if something terrible overtook him en route? What could I do if it did?

"She's a brave woman, though," he said. "Just like Sarah, my own ma."

And he had already told her there wouldn't be a service tomorrow morning anyway, the roads would be drifted full, the neighbors' cars couldn't plow through, even with chains. So what was the use of getting the organ there by then?

"This blow might last all night," Will said to himself. "And then again, it might not. You never know."

What if we caught pneumonia? What if even the Oil-Pull was incapable?

"First Christmas I haven't given her anything," Will mused. "This would be a corker, though. Oh, yes, this would be a humdinger."

What if Ella heard the tractor and that spoiled the surprise? What if we bogged down and both of us froze to death?

My grandfather touched my arm. He was grinning at me again, and his eyes snapped with schoolboy delight.

"Can't you see her face, though, in the morning, when she sashays into that church, and there it is?"

"Can I ever," I grinned.

He beamed, then put out a hand. "Well, partner, shall we give it a try?"

"You bet!"

We stood up, shook on it, and forgot immediately the what-ifs and maybe-nots and the baying of the storm outside the barn and the three impossible miles, forgot being thirteen and sixtyish and mortal. We planned and plotted. We concocted a method, using the OilPull as motive power, of hauling the organ. We schemed an unsuspecting Ella into bed and sound asleep as a ton of bricks. Gradually, as the idea evolved, it took on elements of gallantry and heroism which warmed our backsides, plus bonuses of danger and rascality which shivered us to our boots. And the more we devised, the longer we conspired, the greater the challenge, the bigger the adventure became. It got grandeur.

"All right," Will said, dropping his ear-flaps. He nodded at the ewe and her lamb. "If that old lady over there can have a baby on Christmas Eve, the age of miracles isn't past by a long shot."

"Absolootle, positivle," I agreed, treating him to a little of the latest Philadelphia lingo.

He snorted. "Let's get a move on."

I lifted my lantern. "Full speed ahead!"

We plodded to the house. If, in the cold and wind and snow, we had third thoughts, if our minds conceded that what our hearts had bade us do was beyond our powers, we kept mum.

In the woodshed we stomped snow, unbuttoned and

unbuckled. Will took a lantern down into the basement and I entered the kitchen.

"Well, have we a lamb?" my grandmother asked.

"Not yet," I lied. "We might have to be up half the night with that darn ewe."

"You poor dears. Where's Will?"

"Oh, in the basement. He'll be right up."

She was putting the soapstones on the stove, a winter ritual. Progress, so-called, had already invented the hot-water bottle, and would eventually bestow upon us the electric blanket, but I am not persuaded that these gadgets have been as salubrious as soapstones used to be. They were smooth-edged rectangles some sixteen inches long and three through and weighed approximately ten pounds. You put them on the stove in the evening, and there they absorbed heat. Now and then you poked them about with a lid handle to be certain they were over what remained of the fire. At bedtime you wrapped one in a length of worn flannel, toted it upstairs, and shoved it between the sheets. An electric blanket invests the entire bed. An electric blanket is sissy, if not decadent. But a soapstone needed character. You got into an arctic bed and slowly, with your bare feet, eased it to the bottom. There it burned the night through, blessing only its own locality. If you were weak, and drew up your legs to bunch into a ball, you lost the good of it. If you were incautious, you could practically fracture a toe or fricassee a knee. But if you were strong, and disciplined yourself to lie full-length and wed your body's warmth to that of the soapstone, your reward was a sleep as virtuous as it was blissful.

Will came into the kitchen carrying two tin cups. "Thought we ought to try the cider," he said.

"Won't it be hard by now?" asked his wife.

"Shouldn't be. Not as cold weather as we've had. Takes a warm day or two to turn it."

She pursed her lips. I should note that my grandmother abhorred alcohol in any form. I never knew her to accept so much as a glass of wine. But rather than pursuing the subject she went to a drawer, took out a large ball of string and a tangle of loose lengths, sat down again and began to unravel the separate bits and pieces. This provided Will with the diversion he required. Getting three small colored glasses from the cupboard, he poured from one tin cup into two of them, and from the other cup into the third. He winked at me. He then offered the third glass to Ella, handing one of the other two to me.

"A toast," he said. "Here's to an end of the blamed storm, and a Merry Christmas tomorrow."

"'Peace on earth, goodwill toward men,'" added his spouse.

Will and I drank our sweet cider. She sipped.

"You're right, Will," she granted. "It isn't hard yet. It's quite tasty."

She smiled. He smiled. I smiled. Their smile was a cease-fire.

We seated ourselves at the table with her while she balled string. She would tie a loose piece onto the ball, roll it up, tie on another, so on and so on. I have stated she was thrifty. "'Idle hands do the Devil's work,'" she would say in defense of her industry, but another reason why her hands were never idle, I now understood, was the arthritis. Crocheting and balling string and a hundred other manual exercises kept her fingers as supple as she could hope.

"Let me tell you a little story, James," she said to me. She had more "cider." "It has to do with pride." She glanced at her husband and continued. "I've been thinking. Perhaps it was pride that made me want to give the melodeon to the church on Christmas morning and make a spectacle of myself. I don't know. But the story is about your mother, and what pride can do."

We listened avidly. She had a little more from her glass. We watched her intently.

"When your mother was young, sixteen or so, she was invited to a grand party in Howell, at the banker's house. Oranges were a great treat in those days. If you had one a year, you were lucky, and one in your Christmas stocking made the day."

She sipped a little more "cider." "My, that's good." She tried to knot two bits of string together and couldn't seem to. She frowned and brought the string close to her glasses. "Gaslight," she sniffed. "If only we had electric. Well, as I was saying, your mother was invited to the party, and we knew that sometime in the evening a bowl of oranges would be passed. So I told her to be a lady of taste and refinement. Not to take an orange when the bowl came round. Refuse the first time, with thanks, I told her. Be proud, as though you have an orange every day at home. Let everyone else snatch and grab. Then when the bowl is passed again, hesitate, and finally take one. That's being lady-like. Fiddlesticks."

She was trying in vain to tie another knot. Will winked at me. She sipped again, then began to ball the string without tying it.

"Where was I?" she asked.

She had forgotten both the ending and the moral of her homily. Will and I had forgotten to drink our cider. We were like two tomcats reconnoitering a mouse. What she was imbibing of course was not sweet cider but applejack, a tonic he had turned out by freezing and refreezing the barrel in the back yard, thus distilling the juice of the apple down to its essence. Taken in moderation, he had informed me in the sheepshed, applejack was "as fine as the fuzz on a butterfly's behind." Taken in excess, it had the "strike of a massasauga rattlesnake." He did not intend to get her drunk, only a little "tiddly," just enough to put her to bed and induce a sleep so sound we could fire a cannon without waking her.

"Where was I?" she repeated.

"The party," I reminded her.

"Oh, yes, the party." Her speech was slurred. "The party. Well, sure enough, the oranges were passed, and your mother refused. Everyone was impressed."

Ella dropped the ball of string. It bounced from her lap and rolled across the floor. She lifted her glass.

"The party," I said.

"What party?"

"Mother refused the oranges."

"Oh, yes. She wanted one so much she could taste it, but she said no, thank you. The perfect lady." She stared at the ball of string. She put down her glass.

"What happened?" I asked.

"When?"

"After she refused the orange."

"Oh. The orange. Well, the bowl wasn't passed a second time. I declare."

"Declare what?" Will asked.

His wife rose, putting a hand on the table to steady herself. "I declare. I'm dizzy. I don't know what's come over me. Will, I'm so sleepy."

He was on his feet in a flash. "Let me help you to bed, dear. It's late."

He put an arm around her waist and assisted her to the door of their bedroom off the kitchen. She left me with two words, one at a time, over her shoulder.

"Pride," she said.

"Oranges?" she said.

While he was putting her to bed, I wrapped a soapstone in flannel for her and gave it to him through the door. I returned the ball of string to the drawer. Next I sampled some of what was left of the applejack in her glass. It descended equably enough, but when it hit bottom it went off in the manner of a firecracker under a tin can, with a bang and a clang. I had to sit down. I listened. Ella sang several bars of "We Three Kings of Orient Are" rather loudly. Then she giggled, which was another thing grandparents were not supposed to do.

Will came out and sat at the table with me. We looked at the clock. It was almost ten. We waited, as we had for the telephone to ring earlier, and for the old ewe to get down to business; as Sarah had for Ephraim to walk to the house from the field; as little Willy had for his father to come home from the war. It wasn't long this time. In a minute or two we heard a soft and reassuring snore. He leaned forward. Whispering, he told me to go upstairs and put on a second set of long johns and another pair of socks, and he would do the same here.

I did so. After I rejoined him, we turned the gaslight low, bundled up in the woodshed, lit the lanterns, stared into each other's faces for a moment, searching, making sure of each other, then opened the door and stepped again into the storm.

FIVE

WE WENT DIRECTLY TO THE GRANARY, OR AS DI-
rectly as the weather would allow. The granary was open-
ended at the south, fortunately, for the wind raved from
the north, and when we reached the cavern of the build-
ing the cold and dark were calm, almost inviting, by com-
parison.

First we filled the lanterns. They must not fail us,
and the night might be long. Then, while I held them,
Will filled a ten-gallon can from the kerosene tank, and as
I lit his way through a hodgepodge of implements and
machinery, went back and forth between tank and tractor, fueling it to capacity.

I wish now to describe the tractor in as much detail as I have the Mason & Hamlin melodeon, for if one is the end of my story, the other is the means. Let the reader erase from his mind's eye any image of the modern tractor —a pampered darling packed with horsepower and civilized with every luxury from self-starter to headlights to seat cushions to radio. What I present in its stead is a 1928 Rumely OilPull, Model 20–40, a monstrosity which has not been seen on American acreage for forty years or more, a whatchamacallit which may be marveled at today only in museums such as the Smithsonian.

I begin at the beginning. The front end was surmounted by a four-sided smokestack the size of a ship's, which now and then, according to the engine's mood and the state of its bowels, emitted stinks of black smoke. On its side was lettered this logotype: "OILPULL Advance-Rumely Thresher Co. La Porte, Indiana." The front wheels were spoked cast iron. The engine was an 8×10, horizontal, two-cylinder, kerosene-burning, oil-cooled engine with magneto ignition and a spur gear transmission with two speeds forward and one reverse. Low speed was 2 mph, and shifting into high would hurtle you down the road at 3.2 mph. This engine pulled 20 horsepower on the drawbar and 40 on the belt wheel, turning it at 450 rpm. The rear wheels were eight-spoked and cast iron, with four-inch lugs set in V's for tread and traction, and they were almost six feet high and two wide. Over the drivewheels and transmission was an open cab with a four-post corrugated roof covering an iron driver's seat, steering wheel, and the controls. The Model 20-40 was sixteen feet long and ten feet high, counting the cab, and the whole awesome shebang weighed 12,880 pounds, almost six and one-half tons. Given some armor plate, and a gun or two, and a rotation rig for the cab, it might have competed on fairly equal combat terms with any tank in the First World War. Haul anything in Christendom anywhere it certainly would. There was certainly nothing like it in Putnam Township.

To my grandmother, the OilPull was an abomination of great price—the price being many times that of the automobile she coveted. To my grandfather, the OilPull was power and glory and the symbol of agricultural success. It must have been, however, a love-hate relationship between farmer and tractor. Love it he assuredly did, for as Ella had emphasized, he was "soft on machinery," besides which the Rumely had powered the threshing of every bushel of wheat in the neighborhood for several summers. But hate it he must have, too, as he would have a millstone around his neck, for though he had had no pay for the harvest, and in those cruel years lacked the cruelty to demand it, Advance-Rumely demanded its pound of flesh every month. To me, at this hour, on this weather-wild Christmas Eve, the OilPull was nothing more than a mighty contraption we had but to command in order to move a small pump-organ to a church, a process rather like firing up a mountain to move a mouse.

The catch, of course, was starting it. Everything hinged on that. It was probably ten below zero, the temperature had hovered around or below freezing for a month, and the engine was cold clear through. Tractors of that magnitude were never started in winter—there was nothing for them to do—and although the manual offered instructions, reading, Will had warned, was "a damn sight different than doing."

He first filled the two priming cups, one for each cylinder, with gasoline.

"But I thought it runs on kerosene," I said.

"Well, it does. But gas burns hotter. So we'll start 'er on gas and run 'er on gas till the block gets hot enough to gasify the kerosene. Then she'll purr on that."

He stepped to the flywheel, took off his mittens, extended the handle, which retracted automatically, bent to it, and turned the wheel once, twice, three times, but nothing happened. He spit on his palms and whirled the flywheel perhaps a dozen times, but nothing happened.

"Thunderation," he said.

Motioning me to provide light, he rummaged in a heap of this and that and these and those in a corner of the granary behind a disc harrow and located a blowtorch. Filling it with gas, he pumped up the pressure, lit the flame with a match, trimmed it down to a blue cone, returned to the Rumely and, handing over the torch, told me to heat the glow-plug. This was a dingus extending from the head. Its function was to transfer heat from outside the engine inside, and to concentrate it, thereby vaporizing the gas inside a cylinder so that it would fire more easily. I directed the flame until I got a good glow, whereupon Will seized the handle and whirled the very dickens out of the flywheel, completely in vain.

Breathing hard, he stopped and said, "I have often meditated about the sex of a tractor, whether it is male or female. In case you're interested, sonny, I have decided. It's female."

He stood for a moment in thought, tugging an end of his mustache. "I'm not going to cuss on Christmas Eve," he resolved. "That might put the kibosh on the whole damned thing. But we have one more string to our fiddle. Come around here."

He led me to the other side of the tractor and told me to heat the manifold, which would heat the air taken into the cylinders and thereby vaporize the gas more thoroughly. So I used the torch on the manifold until he grabbed the handle again and rotated the flywheel so fast and so long that if the engine had been a separator he'd have had whipped cream.

When he let go, I could hear my grandfather wheeze even over the keening of the wind outside the granary. I had heard him before, whenever he did anything strenuous. He had what was known as "hay lung," a respiratory ailment common among farmers. Years of cutting and raking and mowing hay away lined the lungs with its dust, it was then believed, leading to shortness of breath and susceptibility to infection. Medicine now knows that dust is not the cause, but rather the inhalation of microscopic spores from a mold which breeds in warm, moist hay. There was no cure for "hay lung" then, nor is there now, except to quit farming.

"We're whipsawed," he declared. "Heat the manifold and the plug cools. Heat the plug and the manifold cools." He stood for another moment, thinking and wheezing.

"We're not giving up, are we?" I demanded.

He scowled. "What would you recommend?"

"Want me to try it?"

"Help yourself."

Full of beans and optimism, I strode to the wheel, removed my mittens, and took hold. By dint of spunk, determination, two grunts and a groan, I gave it one grudging half-turn.

I was mortified. I was also flabbergasted. It was incredible that a grandfather should be strong enough to spin that wheel like a top when a clean-living young man of my muscle could barely budge it.

"Thank you," he said.

"For what?" I was prepared to be offended.

"You gave me another idea. Your arm won't do, but maybe we can use your legs. Here now."

He placed a lantern on each side of the tractor, midway. "Now you heat the plug," he directed, "and when she's red-hot, skedaddle around to the other side and heat up the manifold, and when it's toasty, skedaddle back here and go at the plug again, and meanwhile I'll turn away slow and maybe, just maybe, if you run fast enough and keep 'em both hot enough, maybe we'll do it."

It was worth a try, and for perhaps three minutes try we did, Will rotating the flywheel slowly while I heated and ran, heated and ran, but all we got for our efforts was exhaustion.

We surrendered. He sat down on a front wheel and I leaned against the smokestack. We were both wringing wet. One set of long-john underwear was a necessity, but two, I discovered, were a hindrance. They worked against each other rather than in tandem, constricting movement and requiring a twofold expenditure of energy. Our spirits lower than a snake's hips, we sat and leaned and shivered in despair. His faith in the efficacy of the machine had been shaken. My faith in him had been taken down a peg. I had believed him a first-class engineer, but he was apparently much better at obstetrics.

And then—and then—in the depths of that iron beast upon which we rested, we heard a sound. It was not a sigh of apology, but a manifestation of discomfort, an indigestive protest from its very guts. Will put a finger to his lips, tiptoed to the flywheel, took hold, and gave it one tender, almost seductive, turn.

HUFF!

Combustion!

HUFF! HUFF!

HUFF-HUFF-HUFF-HUFF! HUFF-HUFF-HUFF-HUFF!

The OilPull shook, shimmied, belched black smoke, and we had won!

Hands on hips, we grinned at each other like idiots, exulting in sound and smell and achievement. He had to shout in my ear because the uproar of the tractor was confined by, and reverberated from, the roof. "We'll leave 'er here to warm up! Let's get a move on!"

He had evidently mapped out tactics earlier. Communicating with gestures, we first wheeled the tedder and a spring-tooth drag from the granary by their towbars. That made way for the stoneboat, a crude sled-like vehicle used originally to clear the fields of stone. About eight feet long, it had two small logs for runners, axed to points at the front ends, across which rough boards were nailed into a solid floor. Attached to each log up front was one end of a rusty chain. We pulled the stoneboat outdoors, too, then returned to the heap of this and that and these and those. From it, he extracted two four-foot

lengths of two-by-four, two moldy horse blankets, and a coil of rope. These we piled onto the stoneboat, set a lantern on it, and, leaving the other burning in the granary, started for the house, hauling the stoneboat after us by its chain.

We put heads down and tails up and closed our eyes and tugged. By the time we reached the house we were snowmen. We pulled the stoneboat alongside the steps of the screened porch, ran the rope twice under the flooring, endwise, left the ends loose, set the lantern aside, and laid the two lengths of two-by-four some twenty inches apart to serve as skids between the porch level down to the level of the stoneboat.

We stomped snow on the porch and brushed snow and stuffed mittens into pockets before entering the living room. Gliding the sliding doors like burglars, we edged into the parlor. We had confidence in the sedative effect of applejack, but Ella was female after all, and unpredictable by nature. Each at one end of the melodeon, we rolled it through the living room and onto the porch on its casters. So far, so fancy.

The instrument weighed close to two hundred and fifty pounds, however, and we had the very dickens of a time loading it. We draped it first with the two horse blankets. Together, we hoisted the front end onto the skids, found they were too far apart for safety, had to lower it and set the skids right and hoist again. That done, we let it roll down far enough to raise the rear end and place it. I held onto the high end for dear life while Will went to the low and inched the organ slowly down the skids. There he braked it until I joined him and together we could warp the thing off the skids and onto the floor lengthwise in the center of the stoneboat. We passed the two strands of rope over it and tied it down. I went back for the bench, brought it out, and set it under a skirt of blanket. Then we swung the skids and lantern aboard and set out for the granary.

Had there not been a slight grade in our favor, I doubt we could have done it. Under the organ's weight the stoneboat sank into the snow, while we labored knee-deep in it ourselves. Will wheezed. I panted. We became human horses, asking as much of our four legs as we ever had of Tom's and Dolly's. The tow-chain hurt our hands, even through mittens, and eventually we harnessed it around our waists and leaned into it like a team. I presume it required ten minutes to cover the hundred yards from house to granary.

We rested there. The 20-40 huffed away, running on kerosene and readying itself. I could have kissed any part of that cast-iron monster, for now it would do our work for us.

When we had caught our breath, Will got the bench from under the blanket flap, mounted the step, stowed the bench beside him in the cab, backed the tractor out and up to the stoneboat. "You ride the boat and steady that pumper!" he yelled at me. "Sit on 'er if you have to!"

I nodded, looped the tow-chain over the tractor's towbar, gave Will a lantern, set the other on top of the blankets. He pushed the hand throttle forward a notch, the two cylinders quickened tempo, he shifted into low gear, the drive-wheels dug in, and we were off at last into the blizzard.

It was a false start. He stopped within ten feet and jumped from the cab, bringing his lantern. "Can't see your hand before your face! I'll run 'er off the road! Wait a minute!"

He disappeared into the granary, emerging presently with two S-hooks he'd made by bending pieces of fence wire. Taking my lantern into the cab with him, he hung the hooks from the cross-struts under the cab roof, then hung the lanterns from the hooks, one on each side of the cab, to serve as headlights.

He throttled up, shifted into low, the great wheels revolved, and we were off again, hurtling down the road at 2 mph. The worst was over. We had only three miles to go now, and an OilPull and gumption and Divine Providence to take us.

SIX

HUFF-HUFF-HUFF-HUFF! HUFF-HUFF-HUFF-HUFF!

I liken our progress down the township road to
that of a tramp steamer towing a dinghy over a savage,
wintry sea. The black breathing of the tractor was borne
back to me upon the gale. It seemed to snort a sound
compound of vanity and scorn—vain that it could kick its
heels up in any weather, scornful of the insignificant
cargo it was asked to carry: one rickety stoneboat, one
antiquated organ, two blankets, and a skinny, citified boy.
The cab loomed above me like a stern. I had glimpses of
two lanterns swaying in the wind like masthead lights,
and of my grandfather seated at the helm, hunched forward, squinting into an ocean of white. The next moment

vessel, lights, and captain were swallowed up, for the spume of snow blinded me.

I did not need to see in any case. My duty was to care for the melodeon, to keep it in place, protected by blankets and tied down by ropes. It was no easy assignment. The stoneboat rolled and pitched according to the various depths and drifts of snow. Remember, too, that the instrument stood on casters, giving it an agility which belied its bulk. The only way I could be fairly sure of it was to stand behind, plant my boots solidly, bend my knees, get both shoulders under the ropes, and embrace the organ with both arms. The position was awkward. My arms turned numb, the two damp sets of long johns iced my skin, my teeth chattered a telegraphy of woe. To keep my mind off myself, I projected. We had a mile and a half of township road to cover, with only one hill, after which we turned right, or north, onto the wider, smoother county road which led to Chubb's Corners and the church, another mile and a half distant. Once we reached the county road, I assured myself, the rest of the journey would be a hop, skip, and jump.

The OilPull battered into a drift deeper than most. It slowed. When it crunched ahead again it took up slack in the tow-chain, which shuddered the stoneboat. The melodeon trembled in my arms. I hugged it to me as I had the old ewe's head. I trembled, too, and not with cold. I do not know why, but only then, there, staying the melodeon in night and storm, did revelation of how precious it was, how beloved it had been, alert my sluggish blood. We were removing it from the only home it had ever known. It had been freighted out once before in the almost seventy years since it left the factory in Rochester, New York

—from the village of Howell by wagon seven miles to a young wife alone on a farm, her soldier-husband gone, on a day in April 1863. She had played it, and taught her small son. It was the only tangible link between a boy who had never seen his father and a father who had never seen his son. The son had grown to manhood, and married, and his widowed mother taught his wife in turn to play it. My own mother's childish fingers must have strayed the keyboard, I assumed, her tiny feet must once have tried the pedals. Surely as a young woman she became aware of the instrument's human and historic value. Ephraim and Sarah, Will and Ella, my mother, and now me—the melodeon had been counterpoint to the lives of four generations. It was much more than an heirloom. It was flesh of our family flesh. And now my grandmother, with my grandfather's aid and acquiescence, was offering it to her Maker.

I cannot recall whether at age thirteen I believed or not. At that late hour, on that uncharitable eve of Christmas, it did not matter. I prayed that we might get the melodeon safely to the church. And I tacked on a warning: if He were really real, He had better appreciate a gift like this.

No deity, however, takes kindly to an admonition. We came to the one hill between us and the county road —and couldn't climb it. The OilPull did its level best, but the grade was steep and the drift across it four feet deep. The engine did not stall, the drive-wheels turned, the V-lugs bit downward into gravel. Sparks struck from iron and clods of dirt and a hail of stones were hurled at the organ and me. Will set the hand brake and got down from the cab and huddled with me.

"I can do it if I get a start! Let's pull this right to one side and give us room!"

We unhitched the chain and, each at the point end of a runner, pushed the stoneboat downhill perhaps ten feet. Then, harnessing ourselves with chain again, we hauled it to one side of the road. He mounted the cab and while I watched put the tractor into reverse, backed to the foot of the hill and thirty yards or so beyond. He shifted into second. You couldn't shift gears on the go. He throttled up as high as he could and let 'er rip. The 20-40 tore at the hill at 3.2 mph. They went up like a locomotive, roaring and scratching. They hit the drift with a terrible thud. They hesitated. Sparks flashed and dirt flew. Then they broke through to the crest and I cheered like free beer and the Fourth of July.

He backed down and set the hand brake and we harnessed ourselves again and panting and wheezing pulled the stoneboat into the track and made fast to the towbar and took our places. This time we made the hill as easy as apple pie, and plowed down the far side.

Through a chink in the dark I saw a light wink on at the right of the road. That would be from a window at the Henshaw place, and of course we could be heard coming. A sound as implausible as a Rumely's, at night and at this time of year, would have Joe and Abby out of bed as fast as the jingle of sleigh bells on their roof. To my surprise, we ground to a halt in front of their house and Will descended. I went forward.

"We better warm up! They're awake now, so they won't mind!"

I made no objection. I was as cold as he, but he refused to wear a scarf, and though his jacket collar was up he must have been turning blue.

We left the tractor puffing away in the road and trudged to the house. But no sooner were we on the porch than the light went out in the window. Will knocked, but the door did not open. I drew back a galosh to give it a good swift kick, but he took my arm and led me off the porch where we could speak freely. We put our heads together.

I was outraged. "What's the matter with 'em?"

"Ashamed!"

"They should be!"

"Not about this! Because they haven't paid me for the threshing!"

"You haven't asked!"

"Makes no difference! Old Joe believes in paying his debts, and when he can't, it binds him!"

"Let us freeze out here?"

"Poor as church mice! Reckon they're the hardest hit folks around!"

I knew that. Everyone was sorry for the Henshaws. They had neither chick nor child nor assets, excepting one emaciated cow and eighty acres of the poorest land in the area. It was remarkable they found money enough to buy gasoline enough to drive their Model T to church every Sunday. A local humorist had theorized they didn't use gas anyway, that they ran the flivver on a mixture of pee, vinegar, and piety.

"I don't care! You have to let people in on Christmas Eve!"

"Hurts them more than it does us! We can't let 'em

do it! They'd never forgive themselves!" He took my arm. "Come along!"

We returned to the porch and Will knocked on the door again, and knocked, and knocked, and the fourth time the light went on and the door opened. Joe Henshaw admitted us, apologizing he hadn't known who we were— a barefaced tergiversation if I had ever heard one.

It was practically as cold inside the house as out. The Henshaws had a pot-bellied stove, but the fire in it was low and though Will said we had just stopped by to thaw, neither of our hosts made a move to poke it up, much less add wood. We were seated in the kitchen, on the only two chairs. Three things damped my own heat at the Henshaws: they were even older than Will and Ella, they were small and wrinkled as prunes, and they had no Christmas tree, which proved they were really scraping economic bottom. Joe wore a union suit, evidently his sleeping attire, and Abby had put on over her nightgown a mangy muskrat coat which must have been as ancient as the melodeon. While my grandfather explained what we were doing out on a night like this with the tractor, husband and wife stared as though we must be crazier than bedbugs.

"I didn't give Ella anything this year," he added lamely. "So James here and I thought this would be our surprise in the morning."

He realized at once he had put his foot in his mouth, that the Henshaws had been unable to give each other anything either, and said no more. The four of us stood shivering or sat shivering and twiddled our thumbs till the shortage of conversation became, despite the wind outside, almost audible.

Abby Henshaw broke the ice. "When I was a girl," she said, "my mother would tell me how she used to trade for berries with the Indians hereabouts."

I wondered what the heck that had to do with the price of eggs.

Will pretended he hadn't heard. "Joe," he said, "there's something I want to say to you. We've been good neighbors thirty years. Nobody's paid me a nickel for the threshing, and I don't expect 'em to, not now."

"Money makes the mare go," replied Joe.

"Well, mine'll go a while yet. I want you to forget about it till times are better."

"I'm a man pays what I owe."

"I know that."

"When I was a girl," said Abby, "we used to pop popcorn over the fire in a skillet. We had all the popcorn we could eat."

"Everybody's hard up," Will said.

"Hoover," said Joe.

"If you're in a pinch, Mr. Henshaw," I piped up helpfully, "why don't you ask the county for relief?"

The Henshaws were horrified. "Relief!"

"Sure," I said, rushing in where good Republicans feared to tread. "I'm from Philadelphia, and my father's on relief and we're not ashamed."

Joe bared his three front teeth at me. "We'll starve before we slop at the public trough."

"When I was a girl," said Abby, "I had a dress of taffeta and lace." Her eyes watered. "Mercy, but it was beautiful."

"But there's nothing wrong with relief," I contended. "When you're—"

"Ahem." My grandfather cleared his throat and rose. "We'd best be going," he said to me. "We've got a long row to hoe tonight." He smiled at the Henshaws. "Much obliged for taking us travelers in. See you at service. And a Merry Christmas to you."

"A danged organ," grumbled Joe.

"I was married in that dress," said Abby.

We took our leave. When we reached the Rumely, I hollered at Will. "What's wrong with her? Bats in her belfry?"

"Folks get that way sometimes!"

"I'm as cold as ever!"

"Wood costs! I offered him a cord this fall, but he wouldn't take it! Pride!"

"Oranges!"

He shook his head and climbed into the cab, I posted myself on the stoneboat at the rear end of the melodeon, and we were off again. It was snowing and blowing more relentlessly than it had been when we stopped. I couldn't conceive where so much snow came from, unless some Eskimo had decided to shovel it all out and paint stripes on the North Pole and open a barbershop.

SEVEN

HUFF-HUFF-HUFF-HUFF! HUFF-HUFF-HUFF-HUFF!

We had clear sailing to the county road now, barring an invulnerable drift, and we chugged away at a good hickory, Will steering, lanterns waving, stoneboat slewing, organ secure in my embrace. After a quarter of a mile, lights blinked on like beacons to the right of the road, three of them, upstairs and down. That would be the Stackable place, and our phenomenal passage in the night would arouse Clyde and Kate as surely as it had the Henshaws.

To my surprise, the OilPull stopped in front of the house. I went forward at once. My grandfather stepped down from the cab very slowly.

"What's the matter now?"

"I'm tuckered, boy!" He wrapped his arms around himself. "We'd better meditate a spell! They're all up anyway!"

I was impatient. Dillydally along the way and we'd never get there. And I especially didn't care to drop in on the Stackables, for reasons soon to be apparent. I wasn't tired, and did not see why he should be. All he had done today was milk twice and feed the stock twice and clean the stable and spread fresh straw in the sheepshed and sing a few carols and deliver a lamb and start a tractor and pull a stoneboat and load a melodeon and chauffeur a mile or so. But then, as we headed for the house through knee-deep snow, he staggered, and I had to put my arm through his. He was exhausted.

This time we were welcomed. In bathrobe and hairnet and carpet slippers, Kate Stackable opened the door for us and bustled us in, insisting we take the davenport in the living room, plugging in their Christmas tree to cheer us, and putting water on to boil for my grandfather's green tea.

"Sorry to get you out of bed," said Will, removing his cap and mittens. "Where's Clyde?"

"Down with the grippe, poor man. Chills and fever and a chest cough. I'm keeping mustard plasters on him when he'll let me—you should hear him yell when I take one off—but I expect he'll be laid up a few days. A pity, over Christmas."

"A pity," Will agreed. "You keep him in bed and well plastered and let him yell." Politely he acknowledged the row of tousle-haired girls seated on the stairs in their nightgowns. "Good evening, young ladies."

"Good evening, Mr. Chubb," they yawned.

"You know my grandson, James here, don't you?"

They giggled. I warmed up immediately. They were the four reasons why I hadn't cared to drop in on the Stackables. Clyde and Kate had been unfortunate enough to beget girls rather than boys, and four of them, Agnes, Frances, Delores, and Gertrude, or Toody, ages fourteen, eleven, nine, and six in that order, and arrayed down the stairsteps in that order. I went to school with them. I had no alternative.

If I evinced little or no regard for her daughters, who were as pestiferous as most girls their ages, I liked Mrs. Stackable very much. She reminded me of a stove. She was short and stout and reddened up quickly and radiated a hospitable warmth. She put hands where her hips were supposed to be and addressed my grandfather.

"Now tell me. What in heaven's name are you doing out on a night like this with that tractor?"

He told her.

"Will Chubb," she said.

Her cheeks flamed with pleasure.

"Will Chubb, that's one of the nicest things I ever heard of in my life!" she enthused. "Giving an organ to a church! On Christmas Eve! I can just see Ella's face tomorrow morning! Girls, isn't that wonderful?"

Agnes, Frances, Delores, and Toody nodded like metronomes.

"Oh, I think that's the nicest, sweetest, most loving thing I ever heard of!" their mother carried on. "Say, that water must be hot. Will, I'll make you green tea till it comes out your ears!"

She slippered into the kitchen, which left us alone

with the girls. I decided to let Will carry the burden of dialogue, and began assiduously to study my knuckles, the Christmas tree, the pattern in the carpet, and the ceiling, conscious that they were simultaneously studying me. It wasn't that I was a snob, or a connoisseur for that matter, but when I contrasted Philadelphia girls with the Stackable progeny, the former, as I recalled them, were paragons of beauty, charm, fashion, intellect, and every classifiable virtue. The fact was, Agnes, Delores, Frances, and Toody were hicks. They were about as attractive as heifers and as sophisticated as manure-spreaders. Moreover, they were mean. They had once persuaded me that dragonflies, which they called "darning needles," would sew up male lips if opened, so that for a full two weeks that autumn I walked to and from school with lips sealed.

"Here's that tea, Will." Mrs. Stackable came in with cup and saucer. "Will?"

We looked at him. My grandfather had laid his head back on the davenport and fallen fast asleep. His mouth was open, his breathing loud and so labored that the splay hairs of his mustache oscillated like reeds.

"James. Girls." Kate Stackable put a finger to her lips and motioned us to follow her into the kitchen. When we had, she closed the door. "Here, James you have his tea. We mustn't wake him."

She gave me the cup and offered me a chair at the kitchen table. Green tea was vile, in my opinion, but no more distasteful than Agnes, Frances, Delores, and Toody, who sat down around me, put elbows on the table, chins in hands, and observed me imbibe as though they'd never seen anyone take tea without saucering it.

For warmth, Mrs. Stackable turned on the oven in her electric stove and opened the oven door, then stood at the counter watching me, too, and thinking. The clock ticked as inexorably as ours had earlier in the evening. Occasionally I could hear Mr. Stackable hack and cough in the bedroom, and over the wind the panting of the Oil-Pull out in front. I sipped tea. The girls drank me.

"Your grandad's worn to a frazzle," Mrs. Stackable said at length. "He ought to get his sleep out—he's no youngster any more, you know."

"Yes, ma'am."

She frowned. "It's dangerous for a man his age to be out on such a night. What you're up to is the sweetest, kindest thing I ever heard of—but his health is more important. James, do something for me?"

"Ma'am?" I thought to give her daughters a lesson in manners.

"Let him sleep, and we'll tuck you in, too, and when he wakes up, talk him into going home and bringing the organ to service in the morning."

"Oh, no," I said. "Gosh, no," I said.

"Why not?"

"Because that's half of it, the surprise," I protested. "You don't realize how much trouble we've gone to getting this far. We can't quit now."

"I see." She had hit a stone wall. "If Clyde was well, he'd go with you. And I can't leave him. Do you know how to drive that tractor?"

"I think so. I never have," I admitted, "but I've watched Will a lot."

"Then let me do this. Let me call the Dunnings—

they're just half a mile past Chubb's Corners. I'll phone
Otis and ask him to meet you at the church—he'll be glad
to—and you let your grandad sleep and go on and meet
Otis. Is that all right?"

She had me over a barrel. I couldn't chance anything
happening to Will, but on the other hand it would be a
prodigal waste of elbow grease to forsake the mission
now, when we were so close to success. He had his stubborn heart set on having that melodeon in church tomorrow morning, and so did I, and so had Ella, really, even
though she had seen the nonsensicality of her idea and
made an applejack peace with her husband.

Still I hesitated. I couldn't handle the organ alone.
Otis Dunning wasn't Will Chubb, but he was better than a
prod in the eye with a bull thistle. And in the end it
didn't matter who did the job as long as it was done.

"I guess so," I said.

She beamed. "Thank you, James. I'll go call."

She left us to use the wall phone in the dining room.
I set the green tea aside.

"Don't like it, do you?" said Frances.

"Sure I do."

"Liar-liar-big-fat-tire," said Delores.

"What a sheikh," said Agnes.

"Talk about Harold Teen," said Frances.

"Bet he plays a uke," said Delores.

"It's not polite to stare at people while they're eating
or drinking," I instructed.

"It's not polite to go visiting on Christmas Eve and
keep Santy Claus away," Toody instructed.

"Banana oil," I rejoined, applying the latest metro-
politan squelch.

"There isn't any Santa Claus," said Frances.

"You shut up," Delores told her. "You know Toody's not old enough to—"

Kate Stackable returned. "Oh dear, oh dear. I can't even get the operator. The lines must be down." She confronted me. "Now what're we going to do?"

I resented the pronoun. I was about to say, Mrs. Stackable, it's not what we're going to do, it's what I'm going to do, and I'm going on. To say it with more authority, I stood up and squared my shoulders.

"Mrs. Stackable," I began.

I was interrupted.

"I'm going with him," Agnes announced.

I might as well have been flattened by Jack Dempsey in the first round.

"Oh, no, you're not," said her mother.

"Oh, no, you're not," said I.

"He can't lift that organ by himself," said Agnes. "He's too puny."

"I'm going, too!" cried Frances.

"Me, too!" cried Delores.

"I wanna go!" cried Toody.

"Now hold on here!" I cried, springing from my corner like the Manassa Mauler. "I can do this by myself! I'm not taking any doggone bunch of—"

"James." It was Kate Stackable. She had slipped off her hairnet, revealing the sausage curls she had set during the evening with an electric curler. She had also changed her mind. "James, maybe it's not such a bad idea after all. The girls are strong, and you're really not big enough yet for that organ. It's only a mile or so to the church from here." She looked at the clock. "It's twenty past eleven. I

can bundle them up and you can be back here by midnight and take your grandfather home and tomorrow
morning—"

"We're going," smiled Agnes, recognizing the signs.

"We're going! We're going!" squealed her sisters,
jumping up and down.

I experienced a sinking sensation, that lassitude familiar not only to Samson but to men in all times and
places when hornswoggled by the weaker sex. "But, but
Mrs. Stackable," I stammered.

"Ssssh—don't wake Mr. Chubb," she warned her darling daughters. "James, if it wasn't such a wonderful thing
you're doing, I'd never consider it. But I love your
grandma, and if this is what she wants, why, we want to
do our part. And you should let us, shouldn't you?"

"I guess so," I groaned. .

"You can't refuse, can you?"

"I guess not," I groaned. Will falling asleep, a gang
of insufferable girls barging in on the adventure uninvited
—events were taking too sudden and too dire a turn for
me. I threw in the towel and sat down again at the table.

She sent her four upstairs to dress, and when they
were gone, went to a crockery jar and gave me a handful
of sugar cookies. "I'll bet you're starved. I shoo the girls
away from these, I don't want them as heavy as I am. But
you could use some pick on your bones." She seated herself across from me. "Helping out will put some starch in
their spines—they're much too flighty. You keep a tight
rein on them. Just tell them what to do and see they do
it."

Her cookies were excellent, but the taste on my
tongue was that of despair.

"I'll bet you miss your folks something fierce, being it's Christmas. Don't you?"

My mouth was full. I nodded.

"That was real nice you could talk to them tonight, though."

My mouth was still full. I stared.

She smiled. "Oh, don't worry, we didn't listen in. But everybody knew they were calling you. Long-distance from Philadelphia is news around here."

She tilted her head to check on the girls thumping and clumping upstairs.

"James, sometime soon, when you get a chance, you tell your grandad we feel awful about not paying him for the threshing. Clyde stews about it. But we just don't have anything to spare right now. Will you?"

I finished the cookies. "Yes, ma'am."

"That's another reason I decided all of a sudden to send the girls. Money may be tight, but being neighborly doesn't need to be. And any time we can lend a hand to the Chubbs, we sure will."

"Thank you," I said.

The girls pushed in, swaddled in overalls and sweaters. "All right," approved their mother. "Now go get your presents from under the tree and bring them here and be quick about it."

"Our presents? How could Santy get here already?" a skeptical Toody wanted to know.

Kate Stackable glanced at her older daughters. "Why, he must have come earlier, while we were asleep."

Toody's doubts were not easily dispelled. "I wasn't asleep, and I didn't hear anything."

"Don't fret about it. Now hurry along, get your presents—and sssh."

Agnes, Frances, Delores, and Toody tiptoed into the living room and returned, their expressions something less than anticipatory, holding four identical packages wrapped in white paper decorated with green leaves and red holly berries.

"Well, open them," ordered their mother. ·

They did. Each girl's gift was a new pair of rubber galoshes.

"Well, well, old Santa really knew what you needed this year," said Mrs. Stackable. "Your old ones are just about gone."

"Galoshes," said Agnes.

"Galoshes," said Frances.

"Goody-goody," said Delores.

"I asked for a doll," pouted Toody.

Their mother frowned. "You be glad for them. Millions of kids won't have anything at all under the tree this Christmas—I expect times are just as hard for Santa as they are for everybody. Now into the woodshed and put them on and your coats and caps and hurry. It's getting late and James is anxious. Hurry."

They left us, glum but dutiful. I remained seated at the table since I knew how long it took girls to dress or anything. Mrs. Stackable turned off her oven.

"You're a dandy, James," she said. "I wish we'd had a boy. I love my girls, but they need a big brother sometimes, to set an example."

Her brood entered, new galoshes buckled up, stocking caps pulled down over their ears and scarves up to their eyes. I was about as glad to see them accoutered

for the expedition as I would have been to enjoy a second cup of green tea.

Kate Stackable inspected her troops. "Got your mittens?"

They bobbed heads.

"James is in charge. You do what he tells you or I'll tan your hides—d'you hear?"

They bobbed heads.

"And you listen. Maybe tonight will teach you something about the meaning of Christmas. I've told you till I'm blue in the face—Christmas isn't just getting, whether it's galoshes or dolls or what. Christmas is giving. That's the joy of it. So for once in your young lives you behave, and help, and give—d'you understand?"

They bobbed heads vigorously. I have since learned that unanimity among females of any species is suspect.

She stopped, swooped arms around them, bumped their heads together, then stood back biting a lip.

"Off you go. Don't wake Mr. Chubb. I won't tell your father what I've done till you're back safe and sound—I wouldn't dare. Take care of them, James."

"I will," I said, meaning one way or another.

She catfooted us through the living room. My grandfather was snoring. I'd have given my new pocketknife to wake him and explain my predicament and beg forgiveness for this treachery.

Mrs. Stackable opened the front door and came with us, bathrobe and carpet slippers and sausage curls, onto the porch and into the snow and wind. They must have been even more violent than she'd thought. They must have frightened her. She stepped close and took both my arms in her hands and gripped them tightly, almost fear-fully.

"Oh, James," she said into my ear. "May the Lord be your shepherd!"

"Yes, ma'am," I said.

EIGHT

HUFF-HUFF-HUFF-HUFF! HUFF-HUFF-HUFF-HUFF!

Taken huff for huff, pound for pound, splash lubrication for magneto ignition, the Rumely OilPull 20-40, I believed that Christmas Eve and do to this day, was the most steadfast, dauntless, radiant tractor then in existence and since invented. What it was asked to do it did, asking in return only a pittance of kerosene and a tithe of faith. An ignoramus could have driven it. I set the throttle up, shoved the shift lever into low. The drive-wheels turned and it was on its way once more, smoking and grinding through the malevolent night.

In the rear, riding the stoneboat and hugging the melodeon, were Frances, Delores, and Toody. I had or-

dered Agnes there as well, but she refused, ignoring her
mother's edict to do as she was told—which got us off to a
good, insubordinate start. Instead, she climbed up into
the cab and sat on the organ bench beside me. If she had
been a boy, I'd have beaten her into pulpy submission,
but she wasn't, she was a girl, and taller and huskier than
I, and in the eighth grade, too. So I let her get away with
it, consoling myself I did so out of pity. That she was ob-
noxious by nature she couldn't help. That she had warts on
her hands was not her fault. And that she had to carry a
name like "Agnes Stackable" to the grave—she would certainly never marry—rendered her automatically an object
of compassion. Most pitiful, perhaps, was the evidence,
both in and out of school, that she had developed a crush
on me. It was a hopeless cause, of course. I had no use for
such folderol. I intended to leave a litter of broken hearts
behind me for a long, long time.

We reached the county road. I discovered that if you
wanted to turn at a right angle, you had to revolve the
steering wheel several times. We turned, the stoneboat
followed our lead obediently, and any troubles from now
on would be bubbles. The county road was wide, there
were no hills, the drifts were less formidable, and we had
not quite a mile to go.

The two cylinders settled into a soporific beat. I
relaxed. I must have dozed. It seemed to me I was astride
a great black horse cantering down a road in Tennessee,
saber clanking at a thigh, Colt revolver snug against the
other hip. We were on our dusty way to Strawberry
Plains. I wore blue. I was young and strong and knightly.
The Union must be saved, the slaves freed, and my comrades and I would do these things for Mr. Lincoln and

our loved ones and our honorable selves. And so I dozed and dreamed. Of Sarah, my sweet wife. Of the letters from her underneath my tunic. Of her silent courage when she let me go, and of the boy she'd given birth to. His name was William, she had written, and we would call him Willy. Of the melodeon she played, and would teach our newborn how to play. I longed to see her, and my son, and hear the music he would make for me. I must take my dear ones in my arms, and soon, or die of longing. I could not know a sniper's bullet waited for my breast this very day. And so I rode my great black steed and dozed and dreamed and soon it seemed to me that someone's arms had taken me, and someone's voice was bugling in my ear:

"Dummy! You're going off the road, you dummy!"

I woke with such velocity I almost hit the roof of the cab. Agnes Stackable's amorous arms enfolded me, Agnes Stackable's screech had pierced my ear-flaps. The tractor was tilting to the right—we were indeed rumbling off the shoulder of the road!

I spun the wheel. We lurched left, and regained the level. I breathed again. I was free of Agnes' clutch, but another peril impended. I simply couldn't see. It was snowing harder than ever, and the light from the two lanterns was insufficient. What was to prevent me from veering off the road again, ramming through fences, felling trees, busting barns to smithereens? I pulled the throttle back, let the Rumely come to a halt, set the hand brake, and pondered.

"Whatcha waiting for?" Agnes caterwauled. "A streetcar?"

I unhooked the lanterns and handed them to her.

"Get down!" I yelled through my scarf. "You and Frances take these and walk in front so I can see where the road is!"

"And have you run over us? Not on your tintype!"

It was a wonder to me how, beset by women's intransigence, men could do the work of the world.

"Remember what your mother told you!"

"Ma's not here!"

"What about the meaning of Christmas?"

"Banana oil!"

I grew desperate. Appeals to law and sentiment were unavailing, as would be resort to brute force. That left guile.

"Agnes!"

"What?"

"You like me, I know you do! And I like you! But I'd like you a lot more if you'd co-operate!"

"How much more?"

I knew then that Adam had not tried the forbidden fruit to indulge his appetite. It was to save his sanity.

"Lots!" I proclaimed. "Pecks! Bushels! Loads!"

To my masculine gratification, she jumped down from the cab and slogged back to the stoneboat. In a moment Agnes and Frances, each carrying a lantern, fought alongside and beyond the tractor, and, spacing themselves, began to serve as living headlights. I released the brake, throttled up, shouted "Hang on!" to Delores and Toody, and put the OilPull into motion.

That was how we traversed the last half-mile. The youngest Stackables guarded our cargo, I crouched in the cab, while a few yards out front, only the yellow beacons of their lanterns visible at times, the eldest Stackables

guided me down that howling, inconstant path. Much as I disliked to, I had to give credit where it was due. If it was one degree below zero it was ten, and permitted little or no movement on the stoneboat, Delores and Toody must have been frozen stiff as boards. Now and then the drifts were so deep that Agnes and Frances struggled, slowed, and stopped, and I had to halt the Rumely until they could trample through and wave me onward with the lanterns. Kate Stackable would have been proud of her girls. In cold and dark and travail, at a stop speed of 2 mph, they were learning the true meaning of Christmas— although the fuel which motivated Agnes might have been romantic rather than altruistic.

It was a road we walked every school day, and we knew when we reached Chubb's Corners not because we could see it but because our scholarly instincts told us so. Behind the new church, on the northwest corner, was the Putnam Township ground, or cemetery, and beyond that, a hundred yards or less, stood the one-room schoolhouse. Following the lanterns, spinning the wheel, I turned the OilPull off the road and transcribed a wide half-circle, aiming between two large maple trees and the church in order to come up alongside the stoop. We hit it on the nose. I swung about in the seat, and shifting in and out of low, nudging forward, brought the stoneboat within a foot of the steps.

I bowed my head for a moment. It was done. Hallelujah. Had it not been storming, I'd have whooped loud enough to wake Will a mile away. I set the hand brake, left the engine running, cramped down from the cab, took the bench, and placed it under the stoop roof.

I turned to the stoneboat. Delores and Toody unhugged the organ and got off as Agnes and Frances came back to us with the lanterns. Telling them to stand clear, I untied the ropes and dropped them. Then I pulled one end of the two four-foot lengths of two-by-four off the floor of the stoneboat onto the floor of the stoop and spaced them, by guess and by gosh, wide enough to accommodate the casters. I shouted to put down the lanterns and come close and listen.

"Nice going, you guys! Now here's what we've got to do! This thing rolls on casters! So we've got to lift the front end up on these skids and push it up, then raise the rear end onto the skids, then push the whole thing up the skids onto the stoop! Got that?"

"I'm sleepy!" This was Delores.

"I'm frozen!" This was Frances.

"We can't do it!" This was Agnes.

"I wanna go home!" This was Toody.

"You can in a minute!" I stepped to the front end of the instrument, its protective blankets mounded with snow. "Come on now, everybody take hold and turn it and lift till the casters are on the skids!"

I bent, got mittens under one corner, and waited till they assembled at the other corner.

"Now! Lift!

I heaved. The organ swayed. Then I felt their answering pressure. I pulled and heaved and they must have, too, for with a thud, casters settled onto skids.

I straightened up. "Now we've got to pull the rear end around straight! Toody, you stand up at the front and see the casters don't roll off the skids—let me know if they start to! You other guys come back and get hold of our end and roll it around!"

Agnes, Frances, and Delores joined me, took the opposite corner, and after I pushed snow off the flooring with a galosh, we had no difficulty rolling the melodeon around to line up with the skids.

"Now—help me push till we get it up the skids! Push!"

We strained. We rolled the instrument up the skids till the rear casters stubbed the lower ends of the two-by-fours.

"Now—lift!"

We heaved.

"Lift!"

We couldn't do it. The organ weighed two hundred and fifty pounds, the angle of incline from stoneboat floor to stoop floor was steep, so that we had both to lift and push two hundred and fifty pounds at the same time. I got down on my knees.

"Lift!"

We couldn't do it. I tried to rise. But the enormity of our failure kept me on my knees. My grandfather and I and Kate Stackable's daughters had brought the melodeon three miles through thick and thin. The bulk of it rested on skids not six feet from the door of the temple to which it was to be my grandmother's offering. Lift the rear end two inches and the merest fraction and the deed would be wholly, magnificently done. And three stout girls and I simply could not do it.

I was sweating again, and my back hurt, and kneeling in snow and cold and defeat I lost control. Tears came. I felt them hot upon my cheeks. And that made me mad enough to bite nails. I reared up and threw my weight against that of the organ.

"Girls!" I raged. "Damn girls! If I had another man here we'd do it, but all I've got is damn weakling rattle-brained good-for-nothing damn girls!"

I had not calculated the chain-reaction a few furious words might start. Agnes Stackable began to cry, which set Frances to crying, and after her Delores, and after her Toody. And there we stood, tears running down my cheeks and the four Stackable sisters bawling like infants. There we were, children of the storm, on that hand-made, hard-times Christmas Eve, weeping with such abandon that at least a minute elapsed before we woke up to what had happened.

It had ceased, suddenly, to snow.

The wind had ceased, suddenly, to blow.

We stood there on a midnight clear, in lantern light. Except for the respiration of the OilPull, we stood there at the crystal center of a silence.

We ceased, suddenly, to cry. For in the wake of the wind we heard them, far away at first, then nearer and nearer, coming up the county road from the south. They were not the slow clip-clop which precedes a wagon or a sleigh. They had the rhythm of a canter.

Our hearts stood still as we. Muffled in snow, yet unmistakable, they were the hoofbeats of a horseman.

NINE

IN THE DARK HE WAS UPON US SUDDENLY.

He rode a black horse. He was hidden by a greatcoat, and on his head was a pillbox cap. He rode to one of the maple trees, dismounted, looped reins over a limb, took off his coat and laid it over the saddle. He strode to the tractor and pulled the kill-switch on the magneto. The engine sputtered, gasped, died. Then, in total absence of sound save for the jangle of his saber chain and the squeak of his boots in snow, he marched toward us.

He entered yellow light. He was a tall, frayed man, a young man, but he wore a brown spade beard which gave him a stern, ancestral expression. His uniform was blue, with a stripe down the breeches, and the buttons on his tunic were of gutta-percha. Dependent from his belt on the left side was a saber scabbard, while on the right, snug against his hip, was the leather holster for a Colt revolver.

He towered over the five of us. He looked at the Stackable sisters, who stared at him incapable of speech, eyes over their scarves as big as his buttons. He touched the visor of his cap.

"Good evening, Misses."

He inspected me in an almost military manner, and I stood up to it. I squirmed, however. If the girls had been struck merely dumb, I was terrified to my spizzerinctum.

"Well, well," he said.

I did not know whether I passed muster or not, but I had to set a bold example for my staff. "You shouldn't have turned off the tractor," I said. "I might not be able to start it again."

"We'll see about that, sonny." He rubbed his hands. "Now let's leave off cussing the ladies and get this old pumper inside. You stand guard up there and keep a sharp eye on those casters."

It was an order. I moved to the skids, elbowing Toody out of my way.

The cavalryman bent to the rear end of the melodeon, hoisted, set the rear casters on the skids as slick as a whistle, put a shoulder to the instrument, and with one powerful lunge shoved it up and over the skids and onto the stoop.

"Open the door," he directed me. "And you, Misses, fetch the lanterns."

I opened the door. Agnes, Frances, Delores, and Toody had turned to stone. I got the lanterns and waited by the door.

He lifted the front end of the organ over the doorsill, then the rear end, then rolled it into the church and along the wooden floor down the aisle between the benches. I lit his way.

"Whereabouts?" he asked.

"There, I guess." I indicated a place near the pulpit.

I put down one lantern, and taking the other, went outside, picked up the bench, and hissed at the girls. "You get in there and help!"

But all they could do was shiver and shudder and hold onto each other.

"Oooooh!" moaned Toody.

"Ohhhhh!" groaned Delores.

"Eeeeee!" squealed Frances.

"A ghost!" quavered Agnes.

"He is not," I snapped.

"Then who is he?"

"Never you mind! Come on, shake a leg!"

Finally they put one foot before the other and crept into the church. I closed the door and herded them down the aisle. But they would not go near the stranger, huddling down on a bench as close together as they could squeeze.

He had removed the horse blankets from the melodeon. I brought the organ bench and placed it.

"There," he said. "There." He stepped back and feasted eyes on the instrument. "Good as new, big as life, and twice as natural. Ain't it a beauty, though, boy?"

"Yes, sir," I said.

"Hmmm," he mused. "You don't reckon my note's still there? Let's have a look."

He folded back the keyboard top, raised a lantern, and bending, peered inside the cabinet. "I'll be dogged. It is. Say, that's first-rate."

"What note?" I asked.

"Why, the one I wrote and stuck inside for her to find. Lookee here."

I went to him, and while he held the lantern, squinted into the cabinet. Sure enough, at one side, pasted to the wood, was a slip of yellowed paper with seven words written in ink, a faded brown inscription:

for my Sarah, to keep her company

"Don't know if she ever found it," he said. "D'you?"

"No, sir."

He put his lantern down and seated himself on the needlepoint bench, taking care to put his saber aside. "Oh, I recollect that day. Traded a cow and two hogs for it, and what cash money I had, and would've given my right arm if need be," he said. "I won't so much as touch it, but I'd enjoy to set a spell and meditate."

We were quiet, the girls and I. The cavalryman sat motionless at the melodeon, his long back to us. The lanterns uncovered a rude mural of raw walls, bare floor, rows of unbacked benches, a white pine pulpit, and beside that, the gift of my grandparents. The new wood smelled of sacrifice, the old wood of remembrance. In golden glow the cherry cabinet was enriched, and the scrollwork of the music rack possessed the symmetry of art. What we had come to was a small, poor place, as

houses of worship go, built of pennies and the sweat of honest brows, but I understood then what the Mason & Hamlin would mean. It would do much more than keep the hymns on key and accompany the passing of the plate. The love and loss and resurrection of which it was a symbol would consecrate the little church.

"Have you got a real beard?"

Toody's voice gave us a start.

The man on the bench turned round. "I have. Why don't you sit on my knee and give it a pull?"

Toody was reluctant. "Are you Santy Claus?"

"I might be."

Toody was dubious. "Santy Claus rides in a sleigh with reindeers."

"Sometimes."

"And wears a red suit."

"Sometimes."

"And he's fat and jolly and you're not."

"That's so. But then, I expect Santa comes in many a shape and suit and disposition."

"Anyway," said Toody, getting down to brass tacks, "I wanted a doll, and you gave me darn old galoshes."

"I see. I'm sorry. But let me tell you, Missy, I know a regiment would trade their boots for yours and be glad of it."

Toody was unappeased. "Well, I have to have a new doll next Christmas. A Bye-Lo Baby that opens and shuts her eyes."

"Will you be a good girl?"

"I'm always good."

"Then I'll think on it," he promised.

Turning back to the instrument, he lowered the fold-ing top and covered the keyboard. "How I wish I'd been there, to hear my Sarah play," he sighed, half to himself. "And little Willy, too."

He sat for a moment more, then sprang up with a jangle of his saber chain and smote a palm violently with a fist—crack! The five of us jumped a mile.

"I've got an an idee! Criminy, have I got an idee!"

He reached and grasped my chin in his hand. "Tomorrow morning. James, tomorrow morning, when you come to meeting, you get Willy to play. The song he was a-going to when I came home. So's I can hear him!"

My chin might as well have been in a vise. "He won't," I managed between my teeth.

He released me. "Won't? Why not?"

"He never would. Not after you didn't come home."

"I know that, boy. But why?"

It was difficult to express. I tried to recall Will's words earlier that night, in the sheepshed, when I had put the same question to him. "I asked him why, and he said, 'Because my pa would never hear me. Or see me, nor I him.'"

The cavalryman's eyes clouded with pain. Only now I noted how ashen was his color, how drawn and weary was his face.

"Oh," he said. "I suppose so. But I would've heard him—he couldn't know, but I would. And if he will play tomorrow morning, I can hear. You've got to get him to, James."

He was asking the impossible. "I don't know how."

"Soft soap?"

"He's too stubborn. Why can't I just tell him you said to?"

"Oh, no." He shook his head. "Oh, no." He swept the girls and me with a glower. "That's the one thing you mustn't do, none of you—tell a soul I was here. They won't believe you anyhow, because they're grown up and sot in their ways. They're past believing. No, you mustn't tell."

"I can if I want to," said Toody.

He looked pins-and-needles at her, then at her sisters, then at me. He drew himself to full parade-ground height. "You let out one peep," he said evenly, "and I'll be around someday when you're not looking and fetch you a swat on the behind with the flat of my saber'll make your teeth rattle and your ears fall off."

He meant it, and we knew he meant it, and even Toody did not dare sass him again. But when he saw that his threat had sunk in, his face softened. "Time you spalpeens were in bed. James," he said wistfully, "you'll mind now, give me a song in the morning—turnabout's fair play."

"I'll try," I said. "I really will."

"Good lad. Oh, you're a Chubb, I'll vouch for that. Time to go, young ones. Bring the lanterns."

I took one and handed Agnes Stackable the other and we went down the aisle before him and outdoors onto the stoop. He closed the church door behind us.

The night was still as it had been. No wind gusted, not a single snowflake fell. Over by a maple tree a horse nickered.

The cavalryman dropped to one knee. "Come near now, all of you." He spread his long arms and drew us into a circle. "It don't take a soldier to be brave," he told us. "You've done a fine, feisty thing tonight, as brave as ever I saw. And I thank you every one."

"You're welcome," said Toody.

Since he was leaving now, I thought I'd better ask him while I had the opportunity. "The war," I said. "Was it awful as they say?"

He nodded. "It was."

"Well, was it worth it?"

"Worth it? Worth it! What do you say, boy?" he demanded proudly. "Good times or bad, ain't it a grand and glorious Union?"

"Yes, sir," I said.

"And don't you forget it," he advised, then smiled at us. "And now good night, young Misses, good night, James. And a Merry Christmas to you."

And before we could wish him one, too, he rose, stepped off the stoop, and marched to the OilPull. Seizing the handle, he gave the flywheel a mighty whirl, and instantly the engine banged into loud and smoky life. He might not have been soft on machinery, the way his son was, but he certainly kept up-to-date on the subject.

The cavalryman tipped his cap to us, strode jangling and squeaking through the snow to his black horse, hauled on his greatcoat, unlooped the reins, mounted, gigged the animal about, then rode off beyond the trees, heading south again.

Agnes, Frances, Delores, Toody, and I stood where we were until the sound of his hoofbeats became the canter of the tractor cylinders and were gone.

TEN

HUFF-HUFF-HUFF-HUFF! HUFF-HUFF-HUFF-HUFF!

"Who was that?"

We were homeward bound, and through the commotion of the 20-40 the odious Agnes shrieked in my ear. I shook my head.

"He knew your name!"

I shrugged.

"You knew him!"

I pretended not to hear. I couldn't understand how, when it killed cats, girls could thrive on curiosity.

"I'll tell my pa!"

I heard that. "Agnes, you better not! Remember what he said about a swat of his saber!"

"Banana oil!"

A little knowledge of slang is a dangerous thing.

"He said don't tell a soul!" I roared. "You tell anybody and I'll hate you!"

That sewed up her lips as effectively as a darning needle, so I could steer the OilPull in peace, and down the county road we rumbled, lanterns swinging under the cab roof as we turned onto the township road. It was easy going now, following the tracks we had previously cut through the drifts, the stoneboat dragging submissively after us. The four girls perched on the fenders over the drive-wheels, Agnes and Frances on one side, Delores and Toody on the other, facing me, while I maintained a captain's composure on the bridge between them and allowed them to admire my seamanship.

Lights blazed from practically every window at the Stackable place, and when we halted, and the girls hopped off the fenders, Will and Kate Stackable were standing by the road, waiting. She hugged her darlings as though she had never expected to see them again.

"Bless you, James! See you in the morning!" she called. "Merry Christmas!"

I waved a modest mitten.

Will climbed into the cab, but I sat where I was, in the driver's seat, throttled up, shoved the lever into high, and took off with such a jerk that he had to grab an upright. He seated himself on a fender, and the rest of the way home superintended me with a mixture of amusement and apprehension.

It was a straight run. I thought about my grandmother, sleeping off the applejack, and what she would say and do when she walked into church in the morning.

I thought about the cavalryman, and how the Sam Hill I could ever persuade his son, my grandfather, to try the keys of the melodeon in public when he hadn't touched them in private for sixty years or more. I thought about my father and mother for the first time, I realized, since they had telephoned me, and preened myself on how proud I would be when they heard what I had accomplished tonight. Then I remembered the moral of Ella's fable, and made up my mind to decline pride and settle instead for a big, fat orange of contentment.

When we reached the granary I turned left, facing the open end, and using the expertise I had acquired at the church, piloted the Rumely into its berth. Will descended, pulled the kill-switch on the magneto, and the engine breathed its triumphant last.

There was still work ahead of us. We unhitched the stoneboat and dragged it where it belonged. We put away the ropes and horse blankets. We wheeled the tedder and the spring-tooth drag into place behind the stoneboat. Everything had to seem undisturbed to Ella in the morning. Then we stood for a minute outside the granary and listened to the tinking of iron and steel as the OilPull cooled to rest again till spring.

"Storm's over," said my grandfather.

"Yup."

"I'll wager it's ten below."

"At least."

"Must be midnight or after."

"After."

I glanced up at the stars. They twinkled in the cold and black, but they were remote.

"I'm sorry I went to sleep at the switch," he apologized. "I was just tuckered out."

"That's O.K.," I said affably.

"You made it to the church all right then."

"In a breeze."

"And you and those four girls got that organ inside by yourselves?"

"Sure."

"How?"

I had to be careful. "Same way you and I got it out of the house onto the stoneboat. On the skids."

"Bosh."

"Yes, we did."

"You couldn't have. That's too damned big a load for kids to heft."

"Oh, those girls are strong."

"Boy, I don't believe you."

"You wait. You'll see in the morning."

He was looking at me, but I was looking at the distant, secret stars of Christmas.

"Well, if you did," he said, "I'll be eternally grateful to you."

"My pleasure, Gramp," I assured him with a new and adult insouciance.

We started for the house.

"Hey," I said. "Hadn't we better take a look at the lamb?"

"What for?"

"Well, to make sure everything's copacetic."

He snorted. "All right, if you're a mind to."

We took the lanterns and entered the barn and

walked halfway down the flight of steps into the sheepshed. Most of the flock were asleep, lying around dreaming about green grass and the pleasures of shearing and the mating season. Calvin the ram was awake, however, considering current events perhaps, or the price of wool, and so was the old ewe. She was standing. Her lamb knelt at her side having a midnight supper, its tail alive with delight.

My grandfather tugged at an end of his mustache. I noticed how gray and weary was his face, and how much, if he had worn a spade beard, he'd have resembled someone else, someone he had never seen.

"I still don't believe it," he harped. "Not unless you had help from somebody."

"You didn't believe that lamb either," I said.

We headed for the house again, plodding through the deep snow. We were sleepy and numb and our soapstones would be cold by now, but we didn't give a whoop. We had our grandeur. And what we had done would warm our beds.

ELEVEN

I WAS WAKENED EARLY, FIRST BY A HULLABALOO IN the back yard, then by the realization that it was Christmas morning and we'd be on our way to church soon and somehow, in order to repay a favor, I had to figure out PDQ how to get Will to play the melodeon.

I dressed, shivering, in my best big-city bib and tucker, and went downstairs. It was a dashing winter day, colder than a dogcatcher's heart but bright and sunny. I washed and combed my hair and searched my upper lip as usual for omens and stepped into the kitchen. Ella was simultaneously getting breakfast and hurriedly plucking another chicken.

"Merry Christmas," I said.

"He did it," she said.

"Did what?"

"Your grandfather killed a hen—the first time ever. I'll never understand him as long as I live."

"Where is he?"

"Doing the chores."

"How did you sleep?" I inquired.

"Like a log. I declare, I don't know what came over me last night. Oh, Merry Christmas, James."

Will entered and said he thought we could get to service after all, provided the Cadwells put on chains, because it appeared to him—with a wink at me—that the county equipment had been down our road during the night and broken the drifts.

The next two hours were busy ones, which was ideal, for Ella had neither opportunity nor excuse to stray into the parlor and discover anything missing. We breakfasted on eggs, about which I wasn't particularly thrilled, and on johnnycake, about which I was. Then I did up the dishes by myself while Ella stuffed and trussed our chicken and put it in the oven to roast while we were gone, and dressed the second hen, Will's victim, and packed it in a basket together with some peach preserves, a mince pie, and a Mason jar of hickory nut meats. To reflect that there were two Christmas casualties rather than one, a statistic which might produce panic in the henhouse, made my task lighter.

By the time Mr. and Mrs. Cadwell came by for us in their Model A sedan we were ready and waiting—Will in suit and shirt, although he eschewed a necktie, and Ella gussied up in a cloth coat and crepe dress and little green hat stuck modishly to the side of her gray head with a pin. We climbed aboard, me in back with the ladies, and Will up front with the basket, and found the heavy snow no obstacle to our progress, thanks to chains and the indefatigability of the Ford. There was much talk about the storm and speculation as to whether or not the minister could get down to us from Howell for service—the consensus being that he could, since the county roads were cleared more expeditiously than the township. The Reverend Leon Ledwidge was retired, but motored down to pastor at our church each Sunday to "keep his hand in with heaven," as wags put it. He might have scant remuneration, it was conceded, but because he simply recycled the sermons he had composed in his earlier years, it was probably enough.

Will asked Reuel Cadwell to stop at the Henshaw place, and when he did, got out of the car, and taking the basket, deposited it on the porch by the front door. Joe and Abby had already gone to church. On his return, no one made any comment. The milk of human kindness flowed more spontaneously in those days. Charity then, unlike that of the present, was for the most part individual and spontaneous rather than impersonal and systematic. It had nothing to do with taxes. It was an act of addition rather than deduction.

We passed the Stackable place, and assumed that Kate and her brood had already gone on, too. We hoped aloud that Clyde would soon be up and about.

Then we turned onto the county road. I had minutes now, only minutes, to come to a decision. The cavalryman had me over an emotional barrel. Oh, I could lie, I could tell myself he hadn't really ridden to our rescue last night, that we had wrestled the melodeon from stoneboat to church stoop by ourselves, the girls and I—a lie is often the nearest exit from an adolescent dilemma. But the truth is a better way to maturity, and the truth was, what was to happen in a few minutes the Chubb family, four generations of it, owed almost entirely to the man on the black horse. He had asked me for a song from his son, the son he had never seen, the song the boy had planned to play for him on his return from war, a rendition the horseman had never heard. What matter that out of grief the son had shunned the instrument since then? That boy had become man, and the man neared seventy now? That the father had been laid to rest almost that many years? The cavalryman had asked, and I had said, "I'll try." Try I must, then, and chance the anger and embarrassment and laughter and the psychic damage I might do. Try I must, and trust in Christmas.

We were the last to arrive at church, and it was apparent from the number of cars that there would be a full house for service, a congregation of at least sixty, counting children. Reuel Cadwell parked the Ford, and we got out and tramped through the snow. Will delayed the three of us, and let the Cadwells go in first. It was a ruse, I knew, to be certain his wife would have the full, undistracted impact of our surprise.

"What else did you put in the basket?" he inquired of her.

"Peach preserves, some nut meats, a mince pie—for goodness' sake, why would you ask now?"

"I just wondered."

"Fiddlesticks." And she adjusted her hat and preceded us to the door with a spry, impatient step. She opened it and entered, Will and I behind her, then beside her.

I will not attempt to describe the look on my grandmother's face as exactly as I have described the Mason & Hamlin melodeon and the Rumely OilPull. She must have seen the rows of benches crowded with friends and neighbors, the Henshaws, Dunnings, Cadwells, Deans, VanWinkles, Bradleys, Stackables, Fishes, Allens, Wrights, Teeples, Morans, Murninghans, and others, their every eye upon her. She must have seen the iron wood stove in a corner, roaring with religious ardor. She must have seen the Reverend Leon Ledwidge, white-haired and benign, standing by his pulpit smiling at her. She saw them, but perceived them not. The organ transfixed her. She looked at it, then at Will, then at me, then at the organ again. And the long-awaited look on her face was—language is too often imprecise, but I shall do my best—beatific. Her face itself, for a moment, was young as that of the girl's it once had been. And after that moment, Will took one elbow, I the other, and together we escorted our bride of joy to a bench.

A little overwhelmed, we heard Reverend Ledwidge say he wished, before beginning service, to acknowledge the generous gift of Mr. and Mrs. Will Chubb to the church—a melodeon which, so he understood, had belonged to the family since 1863. Such a gift, he said, would be appreciated by the members, he was sure, to the same degree it had been cherished by its donors. He understood also that special thanks were due Will Chubb and his grandson, since it was only through their efforts

that the instrument had been delivered, by tractor and stoneboat and despite last night's storm, to the church in time for Christmas devotions.

"Reverend?" It was my grandfather.

"Yes, Mr. Chubb?"

"I'm afraid I can't take much credit," said Will. "We got as far as the Stackables', and I couldn't go on. We had a miserable time trying to start that tractor, and then, earlier, we'd had a lamb born. And so I—"

"A lamb?" Charley Greeve was startled into asking.

"This time of year?" scoffed Emmett Roach.

"Yes siree, we did," Will maintained. "I know, I know, but we did. And so I plumb tuckered out. And I think folks should know Kate Stackable sent her girls on with James here, and the youngsters did the rest."

Everyone smiled at Agnes, Frances, Delores, and Toody, who wiggled on their bench and produced demure blushes.

"Then we thank them, too," said the minister. "And now, I think it would be fitting if Mrs. Chubb did us the honor of playing the first selection on the organ. It would be only appropriate that—"

"I'm sorry, Reverend." This was my grandmother from her seat. "I simply can't. I wish I could, but I'm troubled with arthritis in my fingers, and I'd be ashamed of my mistakes. So I hope you'll forgive me if I ask to be excused."

There were murmurs of sympathy.

"Of course, Mrs. Chubb," said the parson. "Then I'm afraid we must—"

"My grandfather can play."

I was on my feet. I heard my own voice.

"My grandfather can play it. Ephraim wants him to. He wants Will to play the song he planned to when he came home from the war."

Except for the ebullience of the stove, the silence was as absolute as it had been last midnight, when the cavalryman appeared. But I could not turn tail now. I had already decided to tell the truth, no matter how it hurt. It was the only way to close the mortal circle, to restore a father to his son, and to assure that son his father had not forgotten him even in death. And it was also time I grew up and ceased to treat two people near and dear to me as "grandparents" rather than the human beings they so stubbornly, inconsistently, passionately were. So speak I must, and trust in Christmas.

Reverend Ledwidge frowned. "Who is Ephraim?"

"My great-grandfather, sir. Ephraim Chubb. He was a cavalryman in the war, and he gave Sarah the melodeon when he went away."

"Sarah?"

"My great-grandmother. And she taught Will to play when he was a little boy. But when Ephraim, his father, was killed, he never did again. His father wants him to, this morning."

"How do you know this, James?"

"Because he told me."

"When?"

"Last night, sir. Right here."

"Here?"

I fixed upon the eyes of the old minister. If I had caught so much as a glimpse of Will's or Ella's faces, or those of anyone else for that matter, I might have collapsed.

"Yes, sir. The truth is, the girls and I couldn't get the organ up the skids onto the stoop—it was too heavy. Then the cavalryman came along and helped us. And afterward, he asked me to get Will to play the song he learned for when his father came home. And I said I'd try. He told us not to tell anybody he'd been here, because they wouldn't believe us. But I don't know any other way to get my grandfather to play. I'm sorry."

To this day I wonder that I got it all out. I knew what I must be doing to my grandfather, and to Ella, too. But I stood stiff as a ramrod, and tried to make sense, because I had a bone-deep conviction that someone else besides those present in the church was watching, or at least listening.

"Maybe you don't believe me," I said. "But the girls will tell you. He was here last night, wasn't he, Agnes?" I appealed.

Perfidious creature—she pretended I didn't exist.

"Wasn't he, Frances?" I implored. "Wasn't he, Delores?"

The loobies sat like bumps on a log.

"Toody!" I cried. "You've got to tell!"

The youngest Stackable stood up on cue. "Yup, Santy Claus was here," she said. "I think," she said. "He had a beard all right, but he wore a blue suit, not a red one, and he rode a horse, not a sleigh, and he had a sword, not a bag of presents, and he wasn't fat and jolly, he was sad and skinny. That's all I'm telling. Oh, and he promised to bring me a doll next Christmas because all I got last night was darn old galoshes."

She remained standing, and might have taken a bow had Kate Stackable not pulled her down and off the stage.

She had not helped. The congregational disbelief could have been cut with a knife. I grew desperate.

"I can prove it!" I cried, and my voice cracked in a new and interesting way. I entreated the minister. "Sir, if you'll just fold up the top of the organ and look inside you'll see the note Ephraim pasted in there for Sarah to find—he showed me last night. He didn't know if she ever found it, or anyone else, but it says 'for my Sarah, to keep her company.' Honest it does. So please see."

Reverend Ledwidge stared at me, then stepped cautiously to the melodeon, folded back the top, peered, adjusted his spectacles, and peered again.

He straightened. He pinched the bridge of his nose. He cleared his throat. "There is a note," he announced. "And those are the words—'for my Sarah, to keep her company.'" He cleared his throat again. "Mrs. Chubb, were you aware of this note?"

Everyone strained to hear. "No," she said, almost whispering. "Sarah wasn't either. None of us were." She shook her head. "I don't understand it."

Nor did anyone else. Men ·studied their hands. Women looked in other women's faces for confirmation or dissent. Children scuffed uncomprehending shoes. The yarn I had spun about a cavalryman on a black horse could be safely discounted. I was a boy, and it was a fact that boys were prone to whistle in the dark. And the jabber of a six-year-old could be attributed to candy, excitement, and an upset stomach. But the note was also a fact, and two hundred and fifty pounds dead weight was a fact, and it was clear to practical farmers and their wives, cousins to the reality of toil and weather and every vicissitude of rural life, that one feckless boy and four

girls could not, unaided, have transferred these facts from
stoneboat to stoop.

I could stand no longer. I sat down.

The Reverend Leon Ledwidge removed his spectacles and polished the lenses with a handkerchief. He put
them on again, stepped to the pulpit, and folded hands
upon it.

"Well," he said.

He closed his eyes for an interminable minute, re-
viewing perhaps the stacks of discourses he had composed in the past, and concluding to his regret that none
of them were pertinent to this occasion.

"Friends," he said finally, "I don't know that it will
profit us to vex our hearts over what we have seen and
heard here. It may be that we have been witness to a miracle. Children have eyes to see things we cannot. And
who among us is to say it is not possible? It is a miracle, is
it not, that in these times, and on the ashes of the old
church, we have built a new? Is it not miraculous that we
have an organ today, an offering from the very bosom of a
family, and brought to us by children? Last night, let us
remember, was Christmas Eve, which has always been a
time of mystery and magic. And if a child could be born
long, long ago upon that holy night, a child our Lord and
Saviour, which of us shall doubt the mystery and magic of
this morning?"

He paused. "Dear friends, let us pray."

We bowed our heads.

"Oh, Lord, we thank Thee for the miracle of the
melodeon. We thank Thee for the courage of these children, who have brought to Thy sanctuary not gold or
frankincense or myrrh but the gift of music. Bless this

good woman, Ella Chubb, and her husband Will, Thy faithful servants, for the generosity and love they have manifested to us and to Thee. Lift up Thy countenance, dear Lord, and make Thy face to shine upon them. And finally, our Heavenly Father, we ask of Thee another miracle. We ask that one of us, a son of man, be generous of his spirit as he has been of his strength and worldly goods. We ask that he play the song his father never heard, and give him peace. We ask it in the name of Thy son, in Christ's name. Amen."

The old man raised his head and looked at the three of us, and then at one.

"Will?" he asked.

My grandmother took my hand in hers, tightly.

Slowly my grandfather rose, moved down the aisle. He stood before the melodeon as though before a bar of judgment, then slowly seated himself upon the bench. He put his shoes upon the pedals. He pumped. The bellows of the organ filled with air. He lifted hands above the keyboard, hands trained to plow and sow and play the iron scales of his machinery, hands which had the night before brought forth a lamb. He closed his eyes.

We held our breath. Time seemed to reverse itself, to tick backward over the seasons. And as we waited on the man at the melodeon, withered now upon the tree of life, he seemed to alter visibly, to sit erect, to ripen into prime, then green into a boy, a boy who slumped in sorrow, fatherless and lost. How long the years, innumerable the days? Would memory fail him? Could fingers do the bidding of his brain, turn the anguish of a lifetime into melody?

He touched the keys. There, in a shaft of sunlight

through a window, tears trickling down his cheeks, he filled the church with music haunting and lovely, he played a song familiar only to the eldest in the congregation. And one by one they rose, the elders, those like him whose wounds had never healed, those who had not forgotten sacrifices made, loved ones lost in fratricidal conflict, given to save a nation. Their voices, quavery but brave, united in historic choir. My grandfather played. They sang:

> *"We're tenting tonight*
> *On the old camp ground,*
> *Give us a song to cheer*
> *Our weary hearts,*
> *A song of home*
> *And friends we love so dear.*
>
> *Many are the hearts*
> *That are weary tonight,*
> *Wishing for the war to cease;*
> *Many are the hearts*
> *That are looking for the right,*
> *To see the dawn of peace.*
>
> *Tenting tonight,*
> *Tenting tonight,*
> *Tenting on the old camp ground."*

TWELVE

I STAYED WITH MY GRANDPARENTS TILL THE NEXT summer. My father found employment then, and the means to put me on a train and bring me home.

Two years after my sojourn on the farm my grandmother passed away, and the half-section of land which had been the family's for a century was sold.

I never saw it again. I do not know if the barn and granary still stand, or the church at Chubb's Corners. I do not know what became of the Stackable girls, if Toody got her doll, for example, if Agnes ever lost her warts or found a husband. I hope they did.

It has been forty-one years. I have not encountered the cavalryman a second time. For many years I disbelieved in his appearance on that Christmas Eve, but I am young enough at last to know better, to accept the minister's assertion that children have eyes to see things we cannot. I trust that in the meantime my forebear has forgiven me for telling on him, and that I may never feel, on my mature backside, the flat of his terrible swift sword. Now and then in cold and dark of night I hear the HUFF-HUFF of the OilPull on its invincible way, just as I sometimes hear, on a winter morning, the antique strains of a pump-organ.

I will never forget the gifts of that Christmas. If my grandfather gave the melodeon to his wife, in one sense, together they gave it to their God. I received a jackknife, which remains in my possession, and a hand-knit scarf, and better yet, the beginning of awareness that no matter what its failings, ours is indeed a grand and glorious Union. Born in struggle and exaltation like the lamb, it has been made from the faith and blood and devotion of those who have gone before us. To it, as to their presence and example, we must be true. Best of all, however, storm and Christmas and selflessness and a horseman out of the past gave me two beloved human beings, not grandparents but a man and woman I could esteem and learn from and remember. These things abide with me.

Will Chubb died the last week of April. He was afflicted with hay lung, the reader will recall, and caught a cold while plowing. The cold developed into pneumonia. The doctor drove down from Howell, several times, but Will was too ill to be moved to a hospital. Everything that could be done for him was done, to no avail. He worsened rapidly. The doctor called for the last time, spoke in private to my grandmother, shook my hand, and left us.

It was midmorning. Good neighbors, Clyde and Mrs. Stackable and Joe Henshaw and Mrs. Cadwell had come by with a cake and a pie and a loaf of new-baked bread, expressed their sorrow, and departed. Ella emerged from the bedroom off the kitchen and said that Will had regained consciousness and asked for me. I went in, to stand tentatively by the bed. His fingers twitched me near. I was frightened. I did not know Death then, that he is no more to be feared than the man on the black horse. He can be kind, time teaches us. He will lend a hand. Grace is his comrade, memory his foe. In the end he prevails, but triumphs not, so long as we remember. And so, thirteen and afraid, I knelt beside my grandfather. His color was gray, the eyes sunken, and his mustache drooped, bereft of luster. His lips moved. I leaned forward, placed my ear above his open mouth. His breath was faint, but I could hear him now.

"Go for a walk," he whispered.

I shook my head.

"Go find the flock. Find our lamb."

"No. I won't."

"Go!"

The word came out of him like a command. I had hopped to that kind of authority before, outside the church on Christmas Eve, and startled, I raised my head to look at him. His eyes reminded me of my great-grandfather's. They were soldierly.

I got up, and stumbling through the kitchen and out the door, marched between barn and granary and down the road, more lorn than I had ever been in my life. I hiked between willow trees through the huckleberry marsh, then climbed a fence into a green pasture, and there, at the far end, was the flock. I walked toward them. I was adult enough now to understand that Will had ordered me away so that I would be somewhere else, doing something, when he died. I knew that when I returned to the house Ella would be waiting for me, and that she would say, simply, "He's gone, James."

It was a lucent morning. The sun was warm, the grass rich, a few clouds like puffs of tractor smoke floated under a blue sky, and the air was sweet with bird song and fertilizer and innocence.

I approached the flock. They were grazing and wondering how they looked in white, having just been sheared of their winter gray. Some of the ewes were fat and would be lambing soon. Calvin the ram scratched his hindquarters against the fence and cast, occasionally, a benevolent glance in their direction. I tried, but could not identify our lamb. And the reason was, I couldn't see the animals clearly, my eyes were too full, and when I addressed them, it was with considerable difficulty.

"You stop!" I shouted. "You stop eating and standing around acting like nothing's happening!"

They were impervious. I began to sob.

"You damn sheep! Don't you know what's happening to the man who's fed you and dipped you and sheared you and helped bring your babies into the world? Well, you better know! He's dying!" I bawled between sobs. "Will Chubb is dying right now! Will Chubb! My grandfather! Your friend! He's going away and never coming back! Never! Do you hear? Or don't you care, damn you?"

It was evident they did not, or were struck too dumb with grief to respond, and I turned from them and began to run and cry. I ran and cried across the pasture and over the fence and down the road and between the barn and granary and slowed down and swiped away the tears with a sleeve because my grandmother stood in front of the house, waiting for me. I walked toward her endlessly, just as Ephraim had left the team and walked endlessly over the field toward his wife in another April.

I came to her, and she put her arms around me, and I put mine around her. I thought of Sarah, and of Strawberry Plains.

"Oh, James, he's gone," she said.

Services for my grandfather were held in the church in three days. My mother could not afford to come, but all his friends and neighbors were in attendance, and the Reverend Ledwidge officiated. Ella played a hymn on the melodeon because she thought Will would want her to. She played:

> *Abide with me!*
> *Fast falls the eventide,*
> *The darkness deepens—*
> *Lord, with me abide!*

> *When other helpers fail,*
> *And comforts flee,*
> *Help of the helpless,*
> *Oh, abide with me!*

She never got her automobile. She herself passed away two years later, of loneliness I have surmised, but she is no longer alone. She was laid to rest beside Will and his parents in the township ground.

So my Christmas story ends in springtime. They have long been reunited now, Ephraim and Will, father and son, and their dear wives, Sarah and Ella, gathered unto each other beneath the oak trees near the church. May the music of the melodeon attend their dreams forever.